DUNCAN RALSTON

SHADOW WORK PUBLISHING

"Bait" first published in *Broken, Battered Bodies* (Matt Shaw Publications), © 2020

Cover art by Intelligent.Art
Tarantino font by Herofonts,
used by permission.

ISBN 978-1988819365

Also by Duncan Ralston

Gristle & Bone (Collection)
Salvage (Novel)
Wildfire (Novella)
Woom (Novella)
The Method (Novel)
Video Nasties (Collection)
Ebenezer (Novella)
Ghostland (Novel)
The Midwives (Novel
In Every Dark Corner (Collection)
Afterlife: Ghostland 2.0 (Novel)
Ghostland: Infinite (Novel)
Gross Out (Novel)
For more, visit
www.duncanralston.com.

This one goes out to all the Woomies,
and anyone who may not know
they're a Woomie yet.

SKIN

1

The two-tone '78 Camaro sped down Mulholland, barely slowing to take the corners, the refurbished small block 350ci engine making more of a choked growl than a purr.

Larry Walker spun the wheel, leaning into another corner. The rocker panels rattled, flecks of rust speckling the road. The Camaro had seen better days. So had Larry. In the '70s and early '80s, it had been featured in gatefold magazine spreads and billboards on Sunset and Rodeo Drive, in Melrose and Fairfax, on freeways in and out of town. During that time, Larry Walker's presence—but above all his giant cock—had covered the pages of dozens of magazines and filled the screen in hundreds of films. He'd been one of the most sought-after stars during the Golden Age of Porn, from old stag film loops to the era of VHS home video and DVD. Now, he was lucky to land a paying commercial to pay his rent. If that hadn't been the case, he'd never have come out here tonight.

Larry glanced at the needle, hovering well over sixty, like himself. "C'mon, baby, c'monnnn," he cooed.

A bright, fat moon shone through the cracked glass T-top, the sycamore and oaks he passed as silent and still as the bones buried beneath Mount Sinai Memorial.

Twin headlights flashed over his grizzled features in the rearview. Stunters often cruised Mulholland at night on motorcycles, reaching dangerous speeds far higher than Larry's Camaro could handle. Two lights could possibly be competing bikes. Was it just another late-night cruiser? Or had that psycho in the mask caught up to him?

Distracted, he took the next corner too fast, bumping up over the curb and struggling to right himself. The redline tires peeled rubber on asphalt, squealing like one of his costars when he'd inched his tool in as deep as it would go. They'd called him the Sex Machine, back then. That or The Piston. It was a term of endearment and respect but often used as a sly insult. In those days he could fuck and fuck and fuck and only the sound of the director shouting "*Cut!*" would stop him. Like he wasn't a man at all, just a hard dick walking on two legs. Like he had nothing behind his eyes but a constantly looping stream of pornographic images, sucking, licking, rubbing, fucking.

The vehicle behind him took the same corner with ease.

"Fuck!" he shouted, slapping the steering wheel.

The bright pink face of his hunter was visible through the car's windshield, even in the dark, its mouth and eyes wide as if in perpetual shock. His years of taking 'ludes recreationally may have kept his mind sharp enough to temporarily escape, but he'd never be free, not driving this rust bucket.

Maybe twenty years ago she'd have had it in her. *He'd* have had it in *him*. Not now. They were too old. Too out to pasture. This creep had youth and wealth on his side. He had a hacienda in the Hollywood Hills set far enough away from its neighbors that no one would notice him coming and going with walls made of foot-thick concrete so no one would hear the screams.

With an enraged boost of adrenaline, Larry slammed his foot down on the accelerator.

The Camaro roared forward. He took the next two turns without risking a look behind him, and when he reached a third, the other car was right on his tail.

"Shit! Come *on*." He rubbed the dash in concentric circles with his long, thick fingers, the way he'd stroked hundreds, *thousands* of clits. The engine roared. "C'mon, girl. Just gimme this one last stretch."

The lights at Laurel Canyon were red.

"Shit!"

Larry had a split-second decision to make. The traffic looked sparse. He pressed his foot down on the pedal as hard as he could and blew past the lights at top speed, narrowly avoiding a motorcycle crossing the intersection.

"Yes!" He slapped the dash. "Fuck yeah!"

The car behind him hit the light on the green and didn't slow. It kept pressing forward, and Larry didn't notice the fresh-laid patch of asphalt in the road until he hit it. The Camaro bounded and swerved. He fought to maintain control but overcompensated—like critics accused him of later in his career, leaning too far into self-parody to survive the unforgiving film and TV industry—and the car spun out, tires screeching.

"*NononoNO!*"

SLAM!

The Camaro hit the ditch and struck a sycamore at high speed, the windshield shattering inward in a rain of glass.

Larry's head struck the driver's window with blinding pain, cracking it. The front end was totaled, the mangled hood popped like a virgin's cherry. The back left wheel spun six inches above the asphalt. Oil leaked in a puddle in the dirt. The vanity plate had fallen off and lay against a nearby tree, SX MCHEN spelled out in blue letters beneath *California* written in red script.

Larry nearly lost consciousness as his forehead dropped against the wheel. The horn blared out into the night but he couldn't seem to lift his head. It felt too heavy for his shoulders, as if it belonged to someone else.

A black-gloved hand smashed through the remains of the driver door window, brushed aside broken glass to grab Larry by the hair—something Larry had done dozens of times to dozens of women—and pulled him back to the seat. He couldn't move. His breath came shallow. A crushing silence filled the space left by the horn.

The gloved hand reached past Larry. He watched through dazed, blood-tinted eyes as the hand turned the keys, shutting off the engine, retracting from the glassless window with the keys held between pinky and thumb. There was a jingle—barely heard over the ringing in Larry's ears—as the man threw them into the woods. The engine ticked rhythmically in the semi-dark.

"What are you—" Larry swallowed, the dry click of his Adam's apple audible. "What do you want with me?"

The man leaned in, turning slowly toward Larry until his dark blue eyes were visible within that ridiculous mask, the one made to look like one of those yellow-blonde inflatable sex dolls with the too-pink skin and red lips perpetually opened in an exaggerated O. The freak behind the mask blinked, as if the answer was obvious.

"We're going to make a film together, Larry," the man

said, his voice muffled by polystyrene.

As Larry lost consciousness for the second time that night, the man in the mask unlocked the door and began wrenching it open.

2

Yesterday.

Larry got the call a little after noon. He was already two whiskies deep, having seen the news early and read the story several times. He cleared his throat, swallowed an acrid belch that tasted like orange juice and vodka filtered through an ashtray, and picked up the phone.

"Sorry to call so early, Lar," his manager, Thom Gorski, said.

"I was already up."

It was true he rarely woke before noon, but today he'd shot up around nine and hadn't been able to get back to sleep. Something had been nagging at him, the tail end of a nightmare or a vague intuition he couldn't put his finger on.

When he saw the story in the morning paper, he set down his espresso—which he always called *expresso*—and broke out the Absolut vodka from the freezer, poured it into a jug of orange juice, dumping in Galliano, and making himself a stiff Harvey Wallbanger.

"I guess you heard about Linda," Thom said.

Larry swallowed another mouthful of liquor. "I heard. You still haven't heard from her?"

The *Times* had reached out to Thom, her manager, for comment. He'd told them they hadn't spoken in a week. Her distraught husband put in the call to the cops two days ago. When she didn't come home a second night, her husband—Chet Daniels, a low-budget shlock horror director who'd been casting Linda Flint in his films for over a decade—decided to contact the press. They were just finishing up pre-pro for his new flick, he'd said, and were supposed to begin shooting in a few days. He couldn't shoot anything without his star, or as he was quoted as having said in the article, his "muse."

The headline read *FORMER PORN STAR MISSING.* No mention of her charitable foundation or the years she'd spent in her husband's "legitimate" films. It was always the same. Larry had seen his friends and former colleagues reduced to the same three-word moniker over and over in the news. *FORMER PORN STAR FOUND DEAD. FORMER PORN STAR IN REHAB. FORMER PORN STAR ARRESTED. FORMER PORN STAR DEAD IN SUSPECTED SUICIDE.*

When Larry had first noticed this, he'd started thinking of his life told in third-person headlines. Former Porn Star Ruins Pot Roast. Former Porn Star Takes a One-Wipe Shit. Former Porn Star Rubs One Out in the Shower. Former Porn Star ODs on Cheetos Watching *Dancing with the Stars*.

"No," Thom said. "I haven't heard a peep. You haven't, have you…?"

Linda and Larry used to date off and on back in the day. They met on Linda's first picture, one of those fantasy ones where Larry was given three wishes and ended up fucking every woman in the film. He'd taken Linda's porn cherry and he couldn't even remember the name of the movie. But he remembered Linda. She'd been a sweet little piece of trim with a ginger-blonde bush and long shapely legs. She'd worn nothing but cowboy boots in the scene and the image of her standing in the pizza parlor set in her birthday suit, even after he'd slept with literally *thousands* of women, was indelibly imprinted on his mind.

Larry got up from the kitchen table and wandered into the sunken living room in his silk kimono. Just thinking about Linda back in the day got him at half mast, his tool slapping against either thigh like the pendulum in a grandfather clock. Given the circumstances it wasn't an entirely welcome hardon—she could be dead for all he knew—but at the ripe age of sixty-eight he took any chance he could get to rub one out.

"No, Thom, I haven't seen her," he said, scanning the shelves of videotapes embedded in the eggshell white wall.

His tapes weren't sorted alphabetically by title or chronologically but by the first name of his most prominent co-stars for easy masturbatory access. Annette Haven, Amber Lynn, Asia Carrera, Becky Savage, Bunny Bleu, Candy Samples, Constance Money, Desireé Cousteau, etcetera, ecetera, ecetera. He found the one he was looking for on the second shelf from the bottom, not their first scene together but the one where the two of them fucked in the middle of a raging orgy, a key party they'd been invited to, the nerdy accountant with a massive dong and his shy yet sexy wife coerced into half a dozen scenes of wanton debauchery throughout the film.

"Well, if you do see her, Lar, call me right away, you got it?"

"Will do, Thom," Larry said absently, the phone tucked between shoulder and ear so he could pop the cassette to the VCR while stroking himself through the silky kimono with his free hand.

"Speaking of calls," Thom said, "have I got a project for you."

"Oh yeah?" Larry stopped touching himself. His boner

throbbed away pleasantly while he waited for Thom to reveal his secrets.

"Yeah. Guy called me this morning. Wants you to read for a part in a film."

Larry plopped down on the white leather sofa in front of the TV. "What kind of movie?"

"A lee-gitimate motion picture, Larry. Not a cameo, either. A *starring* role."

"A lead? No fucking way."

"Yes frigging way," Thom said, matching Larry's excitement, but omitting the curse as a self-professed Good Catholic Boy. "Some kind of serial killer thing. You'd be the grizzled detective on the case. I flipped through the script this morning. Sort of a '70s throwback, cat-and-mouse picture. Think Popeye Doyle, Jim Rockford—"

"Dirty Harry," Larry added. "I'm fuckin down, Thom. When and where?"

Thom rhymed off the details. The map showed it was in an office plaza in Beverly Hills, not too far from Larry's Hollywood apartment. He could walk the distance if he wanted to look like a chump.

He hung up with Thom, promising again to call him if he heard anything from Linda, and pressed Play on the remote.

On the big screen, baby oil-slickened bodies rolled and writhed over one another, genitals mashing, lips smearing, hands caressing. And at the center of all of this, a young and virile Larry Walker and a vibrant, toned and tanned Linda Flint laughed, shrugged up their shoulders, and began to undress each other. The theme of the film was "if you can't beat em join em," summed up by an early line in the film from Larry's neighbor, played with characteristic aplomb by the great Mike Horner: "If you can't beat em, beat off with em."

Larry squirted lube into his palm and took the advice in hand.

3

Tonight.

The scene was playing when Larry awoke. The orgy. Only it wasn't on his TV this time. It looked like it might be an actual 35mm print, screening from an old projector onto a big blank white wall. The room was otherwise dark. The projector rattled away pleasantly somewhere behind him, and if not for the pain in his head and the fact that he appeared to be strapped around the chest to a hard plastic chair set up to face the scene, his wrists and ankles zip-tied, he might have lost himself in the nostalgia it conjured up.

"Where..." His voice cracked. "Where am I?"

For a split second he'd forgotten about the psycho in that fucked-up blow-up doll mask, until the man stepped between him and the film. He was dressed neatly: black pleated pants and a black shirt. A strange counterpoint to the mask.

Back in the '70s, when the ads for them were in the backs of pretty much any publication, Larry remembered his friends calling them Suzie Q dolls or Blow-Up Betty. Neither name fit the freak in the mask, so he thought of him as The Doll.

"You're awake," the Doll said, his voice muffled, yet somehow familiar. "Good."

"Why are you doing this?"

"I told you, we're making a movie, you and I."

"That's what I *came* here for, man. Why did you have to *drug* me?" Raising his voice, the pain in his forehead came back with a vengeance. "You made me crash my car!"

"I didn't *make* you do anything. Not yet. You have free will, Larry." Larry sensed the man smiling behind the mask. "For the moment."

He remembered the horror he'd seen in the basement and tried to spring up from the chair, but all he did was hurt his wrists and legs, pulling against the tape. Peering down, he saw the chair was bolted to the floor.

"Relax, Larry," the Doll said, brushing Larry's sweat-and-blood dampened hair out of his eyes. Larry flinched and reared back as far as he was able. "Oh, don't be so uptight. This is your very own private screening room. I hoped you'd like it."

Larry said nothing. The man in the mask stepped aside, allowing him to see his performance. The quality of the projection was quite good, almost like the original 35mm they'd screened at the 57th Street Playhouse in 1979, with a gala opening for the press and cast at the Four Seasons. The picture—*The Awakening of Mr. and Mrs. S*—had done well at the box office, but had reviewed poorly, called a "lesser, cheaper *Misty Beethoven*" by bourgeois New York film critics. "Walker is certainly no Jamie Gillis," a writer for the *Village Voice* proclaimed. "His acting isn't even up to par with 'farcical' stars like Randy Rockhard and Harry Reems."

"I blame myself for your escape," The Doll said, drawing Larry from his reverie. "I should've known with your tolerance level I'd need to give you more drugs."

Curiosity finally got the better of Larry. He had to know. "Where did you get that?"

"The film? It's the last of its kind, a rare 35mm print. They don't make them like this anymore, do they, Larry? Not since videotape."

Larry didn't reply.

"What you saw in the basement. My *tableau vivant*," The Doll said, with an air of pretention. "Did that excite you?"

Larry remained quiet. On the screen a much younger version of himself ate twenty-one-year-old Linda's pussy from behind. He remembered the smell of it, like fresh sweat and baby powder, and the savory taste, unlike any he'd eaten before or after. Without warning, he felt his member start to throb beneath his jeans.

"It did excite you, didn't it?" the Doll said. "I'm glad. I made that tableau just for you. It's all for you, Larry."

"You're a sick fuck," Larry spat.

"You call me sick. I'm merely a seeker of pleasure, like yourself. If that's depraved, then I'll gladly join the club." The Doll turned and began to walk away. "Relax, Larry. Enjoy the film. I'll be back soon and we can discuss your triumphant return to the big screen."

The Doll crossed the room to a closed door, the clicks of his hard-soled shoes echoing in the large space. He unlocked it, unlatched it, and pulled it open with a squeak of metal hinges. It looked heavy. Impossible to kick down.

"What is this fucking place?"

"It's a shrine," the Doll said, stopping momentarily in the doorway.

"A shrine to what?" Larry called out.

"To you, Larry. It's a shrine to you. Honestly, I'm surprised you haven't grasped that by now."

4

Yesterday.

The office complex was easy enough to find, even with a few drinks in him. Several COMMERCIAL PROPERTY FOR LEASE signs plastered the glass front. Only one car was parked in the lot, close to the doors, but it was covered in a thick layer of dust and looked like someone might be sleeping in it at night. It wasn't an uncommon sight. So many people slept in their cars in L.A. it might as well have been considered its own community.

Larry hadn't driven this way in a while and couldn't remember if this complex was occupied the last time he had or if it had been abandoned for some time. A few broken windows, boarded up from the inside, made him think the latter. He supposed he could look it up but what did it matter? He'd been to worse places looking for work. Often they were in dubious, cramped office spaces above stores in Culver City or the Valley, with posters of films no one had ever heard of covering the walls and seemingly the same blonde women seated in every waiting room, like a glitch in the Matrix, subvocalizing their sides.

Larry shrugged and turned off the ignition.

He climbed out, pushed his longish hair out of his face, and swaggered to the front door. A part of him expected it to be locked when he tried the handle—it wouldn't have been the first time Thom had gotten the address wrong to an audition. But it pulled open with ease.

The foyer smelled like cleaning supplies. There was a security desk with no one stationed at it. Two elevators with chrome doors. One of those folding WET FLOOR signs. That was it.

On the wall beside the elevators was a directory, like in a medical office, with every space blank aside from one. The name of the plaza—JCL Properties Inc—etched at the top. The one filled slot was for AUTHORITY PICTURES - SUITE 201, the company Thom had mentioned.

Larry shrugged again and thumbed the up button. The elevator to the right chimed immediately, the doors sliding open on a mirrored interior. Larry stepped in, checked his hair, straightened his collar, and pressed 2.

The doors closed and the car lurched. He gripped the rail. Above the door, the digital floor indicator flickered between zero and eight like an alarm clock on the fritz. Larry caught a look at his fearful expression and tried to remain calm. He didn't like cramped spaces. The last thing he'd want was to get trapped in an elevator. Especially if it meant losing out on a starring role in a serious picture.

The floor shook, the structure groaning. Finally it settled, and Larry's heart rate slowed as the ding indicated he'd reached the second floor.

The doors slid open.

Larry stepped out into a small atrium with the glass doors to Suite 201 directly ahead of him. He stepped through to a small waiting room. A young blonde woman in a beige blazer with a low-cut cream top sat behind the desk. She looked up when he entered. The interior office was separated from the waiting room by a panel of frosted glass, with a wood door to the left of the desk.

"Hi, I'm—" Larry began.

"Have a seat, Mr. Walker. Jason will be right with you."

Larry sat in the single chair in the room, set up across from a small table with a few magazines on it. He waited, glancing up at the woman behind the desk every so often, not enough that she'd think he was a creep. Something about her looked familiar. Maybe it was just that she looked like every other attractive blonde woman he'd seen in every other audition all across town. Only instead of looking at her lines on a script, she was grinning at her phone. He supposed she could be reading sides on a phone, these days. Less and less he'd see actors holding physical pages at casting calls.

"Have you worked for Mister..." He realized he'd forgotten the director's name on the way here. "...for Jason long?"

She glanced up from her phone. "What's that?"

Larry cleared his throat. "Have you worked here long?"

"Oh." She shook her head, smiling slightly. "No, not long."

Larry nodded. He looked around the barren office. Drummed his fingers on his thigh. "You look familiar," he said. "Are you an act—"

A beep interrupted him. The assistant picked up the desk phone. She listened. "Yes, sir. Right away." She hung up and her blue eyes settled on him. "Jason is ready for you now."

He stood. "I'll just—"

She gestured toward the door. "Go right in."

Larry went to the door. He felt woefully unprepared, no idea what awaited him, no lines to read. Then again, he was the only one here. And the director—Jason Whatever His Name Is—had called for him by name. Maybe this wasn't an audition at all. Maybe this Jason guy just wanted to see him in person, shake his hand. Maybe he was a fan.

Larry gave the woman a smile. "Wish me luck?"

She looked up from her phone briefly enough to say, "Luck."

He opened the door.

The office was empty, just a long conference table with one chair at the far end, near a bay of windows overlooking the used car lot across the street.

Larry looked back at the assistant, then again into the room. There were no other doors. Feeling somewhat foolish, he ducked to be sure no one was hiding under the table.

"I'm sorry, *where* is Jason?"

The assistant sighed, fluttering her eyes dramatically. If she wasn't an actress, she should be. "Go right in, he'll be with you in a moment."

Larry entered the room and pulled the door shut behind him. Standing there in the wide, empty room with nothing but the hum of air conditioning made him anxious. He wondered if he shouldn't have left the door open for Jason, whenever he arrived.

"Mr. Walker," a crisp male voice called from the middle of the room. Even before he noticed the conference call phone at the center of the long desk he could tell from the hollow tinniness that it came from a speaker. The assistant must have signaled his arrival in the room.

"Hi," he said, approaching the speaker. "Can you hear me?"

"I can hear you just fine, Larry. See you, as well."

Larry looked up and noticed the camera in the far, high corner of the room.

"Please, have a seat."

He crossed to the chair, spun it around, and sat facing the camera.

"That's a great shirt. Perfect for our lead detective."

"Thanks, Jason."

"Call me Jay."

"Will do."

"And relax," the man said. "This isn't a job interview. If anything, with your pedigree you should be interviewing me."

Larry chuckled amiably. He felt like he was being flirted with. It was a nice ego boost, no matter who it came from, even if the guy was just blowing smoke up his ass.

"You know what? Why don't you come out to my place tonight?"

"Tonight?"

"Sure. We'll have dinner. Discuss the film."

"So… does this mean I got the part?"

"Do you have the part? Larry, this role was written with you in mind. You *are* the part."

5

In retrospect, he should've known going to the house of someone he'd only ever met over the phone, in an office that could very well have been broken into just to set up the conference call, with an assistant that could've been hired for the day, was a bad idea.

Unfortunately, the ego boost and the thought of landing a lead role in a legitimate film made him careless, and when the gates rolled open at the estate in the Hollywood Hills seemingly of their own accord—though Larry could see the camera pointing down at him, perched on a high pole—he realized he still didn't know the director's last name.

He could very easily disappear in a place like this and no one would even know. People disappeared in this city all the time. He remembered reading a stat like twenty-five thousand adults and children went missing in L.A. County every year. Some people *came* here to disappear.

Larry glanced at his watch. Just after eight. This deep into October, the sun had already set hours ago. It wasn't quite dark—L.A. never got *full* dark, not without a major blackout—but it was dark enough to be sinister. He never drove out to the Hills at night. If he went anywhere after dark it was usually to some club in West Hollywood or the Fashion District.

Should probably put in a call to Thom. Let him know I got the part.

"*Park in front of the house*," came Jason's voice from the speaker beside the gate, making Larry fumble and drop his phone. It bounced off the passenger seat and landed in a heap of discarded fast-food bags, cups and crumpled receipts, along with dozens of flyers and business cards he'd found stuck in various places on his car a couple of times a week.

"*You haven't changed your mind, have you?*" the voice on the speaker said. It only now just occurred to him he still hadn't seen this guy's face.

"Nope, just..." Larry glanced down at the junk in the passenger footwell. He was about to add, *dropped my phone*, but said instead, "Be right up." He was already a few minutes late. Best not to keep the man waiting.

He touched the gas, and the Camaro lurched forward between the gates, gravel crunching. Driving slow down the long drive lined with tall trees, he watched in the rearview as they rolled shut behind him.

The house, when it emerged from behind the trees, looked like a jumble of light and dark children's blocks inlaid with horizontal rectangular slots of glass for windows, seemingly at random, from which a bright white light shone through. It looked like some kind of Brutalist alien spacecraft landed in the woods. Thinking about that reminded him of the *E.T.* porn parody he'd done in the '80s. He'd worn a store-bought E.T. mask and screwed Elliot's (adult) sister, his mother, and half of the scientists trying to study him. His catchphrase, uttered in the weird raspy goat-like voice he'd used for the character, was "E.T., bone ho." Amblin had sued and the film had been barred from release.

Larry pulled up behind a shiny black Audi parked in front of the odd-shaped structure and turned off the engine. He shoved the keys in the tight front pocket of his jeans and stepped out of the car.

The night was cool, the warmth and smog of the day cleared, the air perfumed with sage and jasmine. The Hills always smelled like a classy lady at night—except in the few weeks leading up to the winter rainy season, when gardeners sprinkled the lawns with manure. She didn't smell quite so classy then. She smelled like shit.

Larry checked himself out in the cracked side mirror, smoothed his bangs to the side and straightened his collar, then casually strode up the steps to the front door.

He thumbed the buzzer. A musical chime echoed through the house. Through the vertical slot of frosted glass in the door, he saw a dark shape moving toward it. A moment later, the door opened.

A man slightly taller than Larry's five-foot-ten stood in the door, gazing at him. He was dressed neatly in a black blazer and plain black shirt, with black pleated pants, his dark hair swept back from a receded hairline. His lower jaw was long, making the lower half of his face look somewhat gaunt, but his eyes were bright and inquisitive, his complexion shiny, healthy-looking.

"Come in, Mr. Walker." The voice didn't match what Larry had heard from either speaker today, again putting him off kilter. There was a slight Britishness to it. "Jason's expecting you."

Larry stepped across the threshold. "Thanks, uh…"

"Reed," the man said. "I'm Jason's… well, I suppose you'd call me his butler, though we never use the term."

"Right on," Larry said.

"Have a seat in the drawing room, please." Reed gestured toward the sofas and chairs set up in front of a roaring stone fireplace.

"Sure thing." Larry stopped a few steps into the foyer, glancing down at his vintage Tony Lama snakeskin boots. "Should I take off my shoes?"

"Don't worry about it," the butler said, the corners of his eyes wrinkling, though he wasn't smiling. "In fact, he'd prefer you leave your boots on."

"Great," Larry said, though it did seem like an odd thing to mention. Maybe it was part of the character.

"I was just leaving for the night," the butler said. "But please, make yourself at home. Pour yourself a drink. Harvey Wallbanger, that's your drink of choice, isn't it? I've added Galliano and Absolut to the bar."

"Rock on. Thanks, brother."

Reed smiled lightly. "Don't thank me, Mr. Walker. Good night," he said, and stepped out into the night, closing the door behind him.

Larry wandered into the drawing room—it made him feel silly and pretentious just thinking that word—his bootheels echoing in the large space. Rich people really liked to flash it in your face how much money they had. The ceilings were always high, the rooms large with very little furniture to take up space. The homes of the rich and famous were more like fashionable boutiques. You could throw a party in a single room, mingle the entire night, and still not meet everyone who'd attended.

Quit being jealous, he thought. *If you had this kinda money you'd be living like Rocky in* Rocky II. *Have your own robot butler.*

He chuckled and looked over the various animal heads on plaques and full sauntered over to check out the bar.

Outside the Audi's headlights came on. He couldn't hear the engine. Whether that was a testament to the car or the soundproofing of the house, he wasn't sure. Regardless, Larry figured the butler must be paid handsomely to afford a car like that. Larry's net worth was sometimes estimated at upwards of a million dollars on the internet, but even he couldn't afford to drive around a car like that. In truth, he had some money tucked away in stocks and bonds but he needed to keep working to pay the bills. The guy who owned this house probably had enough wealth to be passed down for *generations*.

The Audi's taillights cast their red glow over the trees as it ambled down the drive. Soon even they weren't visible, and Larry was left alone in a stranger's mansion—although he supposed he wasn't *entirely* alone. Jason was here somewhere. It was only a matter of *when* he'd make his appearance.

Larry fished out two ice cubes from a silver dish with a pair of small silver tongs, dropped them into a tall glass, poured from a crystal decanter what he assumed from the smell was vodka onto the ice, then the Galliano. He'd just reached for the jug of chilled orange juice, condensation dripping from the glass, when a sound caught his attention.

He paused with his fingers hovering near the handle, listening.

Larry just about gave up but the sound came again. This time he heard it more clearly. It sounded like a voice, from somewhere inside the house. A child, or a woman with a particularly high voice.

Maybe Jaybird's gettin laid, the old dog.

He grinned, dismissing the sound. He poured some juice into the glass, and shook it around as he returned to the sofas. They were hard and uncomfortable, nothing like what he was expecting a rich person's furniture to feel like. If he ever got rich—won the lottery, for instance—he'd make damn sure the seating *pampered* his guests asses. This was like sitting on slightly spongy boxes.

Where the hell is this guy? I mean, you tell me to be here at a certain time, and I'm here fuckin late, and you're still upstairs balling some bimbo with a voice like Minnie Mouse? Finish up already and—

"*...ah...*"

Larry stood up ramrod straight from the sofa, the contents of his glasses spilling over his hand. That one *definitely* sounded like a muted scream. And not a good scream. Not an *I'm-about-to-cum* scream.

It sounded like a scream of terror.

Okay, fuck this place.

Larry placed the Wallbanger on a coaster on the glass table and crossed the room to the door.

"I'm outta here. I don't need this shit that bad."

The scream came again as he passed an open doorway. It led into a room he hadn't noticed when he'd entered the foyer. He stepped through, marveling at a dozen animal heads mounted on the walls, from deer to a pair of lions to a white rhino. A gray wolf stalked a caribou, both animals mounted on pedestals. A cheetah bared its fangs at an owl. A black stallion stood frozen in mid-trot across the room, its mane cascading back over its withers as if caught in the wind. Every animal was perfectly preserved, such flawless representations of their live counterparts in the wild they could've belonged to a museum.

Larry reached out and stroked the horse's flank. It was equally smooth and bristly, like Dimples, the horse he'd ridden as a child. They weren't statues or replicas: they were taxidermied, all of these animals. Their hides and feathers and fur stuffed with sawdust or cotton and shaped with armatures.

When he was a little kid he'd loved animals. His uncles had been hunters, and he'd convinced one of them to save him a strip of deer fur, which he'd stroked lovingly every now and then for months, rubbing it against his cheeks and skin, until the strip of fur was as ragged as an animal with mange.

"*...ah...*"

The sound startled him. He'd been so absorbed in his memories and the sight before him he'd nearly forgotten what had drawn him in here in the first place. At the far end of the taxidermy room, a set of white stairs wound down into what he assumed was a basement or wine cellar. The voice appeared to be coming from there.

"Fuck," he muttered, already aware he was going down those stairs whether he wanted to or not. If someone was getting hurt down there, if some kind of casting couch bullshit was going on, he wasn't about to walk away and let it happen. "Fucking fuck."

He crept to the stairs, wary of every creak and groan his boots made on the wood floor. At the top of the stairs he peered down. He couldn't see around the column. The walls were painted a flat white, but unlike the pristineness of the other walls on the first floor, the flaws in the plaster became visible as it descended into the dark.

The scream came again. This time it was a word.

"*...help...*"

Larry suppressed the urge to run down the rest of the way and crept as slowly as possible to avoid being heard. His own heartbeat thudded in his ears.

Shit, this is just like outta one of Chet's movies. Oughta pitch it to him next time I see him and Linda.

He'd been thinking about Linda most of the day but her disappearance had slipped his mind after the thing at the office. He tried not to think it, but the thought came anyway: *If I ever see them again.*

Christ, she could be dead...

The stairwell ended at a short corridor. Opposite the stairs was a single heavy door, locked and bolted. To the left the hall opened on what appeared to be a vast, dark space. The urge to shout just to see if it would echo nearly overcame him.

"*...AH...*"

There it was again, much louder this time. His eyes had adjusted to the light and now what looked like two giant cubes were just barely visible to the right and left of him. The sound appeared to be coming from the one on the left.

What the fuck is this Joe Goldberg shit?

Larry crossed to it, reaching out ahead of him so he wouldn't walk into something he couldn't see. When his fingers touched a smooth, cool surface they made a hollow plunking sound, like tapping an empty fish tank.

Glass.

"*...AH...*"

It was so close to him now, maybe a foot away. It was odd how steady they came. The space between them almost seemed like the sound was on a loop.

His fingers danced across the glass until they reached a different surface. Cooler with striations. Plaster, maybe.

Cement.

He slid the hand down the—column, pillar—until they found a switch.

"*...AH...*"

Do I really want to see what's in there?

He didn't, but he had to know what was making the sound. If someone was in there, if someone was *hurt*—he couldn't leave without doing something.

He flicked the switch.

The inside of the cube illuminated. The wall was indeed glass, the columns cement.

Larry took a step back in surprise.

Within was a set made to look like a doctor's office from the '70s or '80s, with all kinds of medical drawings and posters on the wood paneling. In the middle of this was a woman in a hospital gown seated in a gynecology chair, her legs spread with her feet in the stirrups. On the floor between her legs, some kind of robotic piston arm thrust a dildo in and out of the woman's vagina. Her eyes were wide and glassy, apparently staring at him as the dildo rammed in and out, her mouth open in an "O" of apparent pleasure.

It looked like some kind of pornographic art exhibit, reminding Larry of the Endangered Species section of the Natural History Museum he hadn't visited since the '90s. The colors seemed to pop, especially the rosiness of the woman's cheeks and pussy lips, the mint green hospital gown, and her bright blonde hair in a teased Farrah Fawcett look.

The sound of her moans assaulted him suddenly from a speaker below the switch: "*...AH... AH... AH...*"

Now the sound made sense, but it seemed off from what he was seeing, like an old porn reel with the sound out of synch. The O of her lips widened and reduced slightly out of time with the moans. An untrained eye might not have caught it. Having dubbed dozens of porn films before the industry switched to VHS, Larry noticed it right away. The effect was unsettling.

What's going on here? Some kind of kinky submissive shit?

The dildo pistoned. The woman in the chair moaned. Larry felt himself beginning to stretch out the right thigh of his jeans. Her glossy eyes looked dazed, either out of her head with ecstasy or drugs.

She can't see me. She's looking right at me... but she can't see me. Gotta be one-way glass.

Unaware he was doing so, Larry began stroking his cock through his jeans. Up and down the length of it, matching the rhythm of the dildo plunging in and out of her pussy. In and out, up and down.

"*Larry, look out—!*"

Larry turned toward the voice, somewhere in the dark beyond the cube.

Before he could investigate, he felt a sharp sting in his neck, and a gloved hand smelling of clean leather gripped him around the nose and mouth. He tried to fight but the effect of whatever he'd been stuck with was immediate. The light began to dwindle around scene in the cube, like an old vignette fade to black.

It only occurred to him as his lights went completely out that the scene in the cube was from one of his movies. And not just a random film, either: it was *The Awakening of Mr. and Mrs. S*, the one he'd been watching that very morning.

6

Now.

The memory of the drugged woman in the basement came back to Larry as The Doll closed and bolted the door behind himself. The drugs must have messed with his short-term memory, like a drunken blackout. He remembered the whole thing now, but just bits and pieces from when the needle pierced his neck to when he woke up here in the chair.

A highlight reel of the time in between played out in his mind now: waking briefly as the leather-gloved man—obviously The Doll—dragged him up the stairs, and again as he sat him in a chair—*this* chair—in the screening room. The sound of The Doll humming behind him as he set up the projector. Then leaping up from the chair with a sudden burst of fear-fueled adrenaline, flashes of running through a maze of endless white hallways, finding himself back in the drawing room somehow, then outside, then behind the wheel of the Camaro.

His mind had started to clear once he was driving. He remembered the gates coming open as he neared them, thinking they must be automated but not caring to think too deeply about it, just blowing through them as fast as the Camaro would allow. Everything after that was fresh in his memory, despite the head injury, until he blacked out while The Doll tore the car door open.

From there, he'd woken up here, with the last reel of *Mr. and Mrs. S* playing on a loop.

The Doll wanted him to make a film. Judging by what the psycho had said before he left the room—claiming this place was some sort of *shrine* to him—and what he'd seen in the basement, the recreation of the expectant mother scene from *Mr. and Mrs. S*, with the pistoning dildo in the place of Larry's own member, he had a pretty good idea what kind of picture they'd be making.

Larry didn't suspect it was a detective movie, no matter what script he'd sent Thom.

Whatever the script had been, it was merely bait. The Doll—was his real name even Jason?—knew Larry was looking for work in legitimate films. It was common knowledge, particularly to someone who appeared to be a fan of his work. The office space was likely a front, either rented for the day or broken into. The assistant was likely an actor, as he'd suspected he remembered her face from some audition or another. It was even possible they'd worked together on some commercial or film background.

Lure him in with a promise of work. Switch the location to somewhere not communicated through the manager. Lull him into a false sense of security with the butler—likely another actor—and the Harvey Wallbanger.

Then what? Did he *want* Larry to find the woman in the basement? Was that bait, too? Did he want him to witness his devotion to Larry's career, or at least to that film? Did he *let* him escape?

Was all of this part of the performance?

Is he filming me right now?

Larry wrenched his head around as far as it would go in both directions. He didn't see any cameras, but the flickering light from the projector was too bright to see all the way back into the far corners. It was possible an entire crew was back there in the dark, filming him, though he had to admit even at his most paranoid as he was now, it wasn't very likely.

So, The Doll wanted him to make a skin flick, a porno. He'd quit the business a decade ago, when he'd started having to take boner pills just to keep from going soft mid-shot. Not much more embarrassing to a man who was once a legitimate "woodsman"—which in the business meant he could command an erection at will—than trying to cram his semihard dick into someone's asshole on camera while an entire crew watched and waited. After a while, the pills had started to give him concerning palpitations and vision loss, and sent him to the emergency room twice for priapism, so he'd quit taking them and left the industry.

But he *could* take the pill and fuck whoever he needed to fuck if it meant it would save his life.

The only real concern was just who—or *what*—The Doll wanted him to fuck.

He'd seen *A Serbian Film*, the brutal tale of a faded porn star like himself, although much younger, paid to star in an art house film which ends up being a snuff tape. The director drugs him and tricks him into having sex with his own young son. It was shocking and disturbing and Larry had walked out halfway through the screening—the baby rape scene had been the final straw—at a party with some of the more unsavory elements in the gonzo porn market, who'd been laughing and cheering during the worst parts. It seemed like some of them had seen it multiple times.

There was no way he'd fuck a kid. Bad enough that he'd worked with Traci Lords when she was underage, but at least she'd been in her late teens.

He wasn't fucking animals, either. No zoophilia or bestiality or whatever fancy name they wanted to give it. Not barnyard animals or domesticated. Judging by the taxidermy room he'd seen earlier, it was obvious The Doll had an obsession with them. Larry had experienced a close call in the '80s, when a director paid to fly him out to Spain, where it turned out he'd wanted him to star in a film where the actors were fucking sheep and pigs. Just the smell of these animals when he'd walked on set was atrocious, a musky odor he couldn't get out of his nostrils for days, no matter how much coke he'd snorted afterwards to obliterate the memory. He'd seen one of the farmers, he guessed, going around with a broom and a dustpan cleaning up their shit, while one of the background actors spit into his hand and slathered up his dick, gripping an animal's tail. Larry had found the director, told him to fuck them himself and stormed off set. He'd gotten on the next flight back to the States and never gone back to Europe, not even when he'd been nominated for a Ninfa award and the Hot d'Or for Best American Actor almost a decade later.

But… if the director had put a gun to his head back then… he supposed he would have had to grin and bear it. With a gun to his head, he'd probably fuck just about anything.

No gun had been produced here yet. It was possible there wouldn't ever *be* a gun. The Doll hadn't threatened him with violence. But he'd been drugged and kidnapped. He'd been strapped and zip-tied to a chair. The implication of violence bubbled under the surface of every detail, every word.

On the screen, his and Linda's younger selves shrugged up their shoulders and undressed each other, choosing to join the orgy their friends, colleagues and neighbors wouldn't let them ignore.

Wait a second, hang on a damn minute… a woman called out for me down there, right before he stuck me with the needle. Called me by name. *Told me to look out. I knew I recognized the gynecology scene but that voice was familiar, too. Fuck me…*

The revelation hit him like the strike of a match. Down in the basement, possibly in another of the glassed-in cement cubes he'd seen in the dark, Linda Flint was trapped just like he was.

7

Larry had to piss.

The Doll let the film run three more times before the latches unlocked and the door came swinging open once again. By then Larry had been calling out for at least half the film, on the verge of pissing his pants.

"Please. I gotta piss real bad, man."

The Doll cocked his head. "So piss."

"I'm not pissing my pants."

"Then you're going to have to learn self-control. It's been a long time since you were in the industry. When was the last time you exercised your pubococcygeus muscle?"

"My what? What the fuck are you talking about, man?"

"Your PC muscles, Larry. When was the last time you did Kegels?"

"Kegels? Isn't that for chicks?"

"Larry. A good manager would have informed you, if you'd done regular Kegels you never would have needed to take those awful pills to keep an erection. You'd still be at the top of the industry."

"Great! That's really helpful! Now can I please just use the bathroom?"

The Doll remained silent, then stepped around him, out of sight. The sound of something hollow and metallic scraped on cement. He returned with a bedpan, which he placed on the floor between Larry's feet.

Larry jerked his arms and wriggled his fingers. The zip ties were tight enough to cut off much of his circulation, giving him pins and needles. "Cut my hands free, man."

"I'm afraid I can't do that."

"What? How am I supposed to piss?"

"You'll just have to trust me. Do you trust me, Larry?"

Fuck no, I don't trust you, his mind screamed. But he said, "Sure. Okay. I trust you."

The Doll reached for his zipper.

Larry pulled his hips back as far as they would go. He wasn't a homophobe. He'd done some gay-for-pay flicks in the '80s, and while it wasn't really his thing he'd had a bit of fun and made some cash. But the thought of this psycho getting anywhere near his dick inspired nothing but terror.

What do I do if he tries to jerk me off? What if he tries to crush my balls?

The Doll blinked behind the mask. "You said you trust me. Let me help you."

Larry relaxed his hips. The Doll grasped his zipper with a gloved hand and jerked it down. The anticipation of finally being allowed to empty his bladder made his back teeth hurt. The Doll reached into Larry's pants and grasped his cock around the root. He pulled it out and let it hang over the edge of the chair. Then he picked up the bedpan.

"Okay, Larry. You can urinate now."

Larry let loose. The urine splashed the pan with the sound of a power washer spraying empty paint cans. He sighed heavily, his whole body relaxing into the stream leaving his body.

"I'm going to take the pan away, Larry. If you piss on the floor, even one single drop, I will hurt you."

"What? Dude, you can't—"

"One... two..." On three, the Doll pulled the bedpan away. Larry tensed immediately, clenching as hard as he could to stem the flow. But he was in his sixties. He couldn't even use the toilet on a regular visit without two or three drops staining the inside of his undershorts. It was bound to drip at least once or twice.

He didn't want to find out what The Doll would do to him if that happened.

God, please, suck that piss right back up into my dick.

"Very good," The Doll said, returning the bedpan to its position below Larry's penis. "Okay, you can finish now."

Larry let the last of the urine out in a torrent, gasping audibly. When he was finished, The Doll placed it on the floor and tucked Larry's cock back into his jeans.

"You see? Self-control. I knew you had it in you."

"Yeah, great. Thanks."

The Doll stood with the bedpan, its dark yellow contents sloshing. "Looks like you'll need some hydration. I'll get you some water. Do you like LaCroix?"

Larry hated sparkling water and didn't understand the obsession with it, but he nodded, if only to get some moisture in his body.

"Very well. One LaCroix for my star coming right up."

The Doll turned with the bedpan and headed for the door.

"Jason?" Larry called out.

The man stopped in his tracks but didn't turn.

"Yes, Larry?"

"Who's the woman in the basement?"

"Which woman, Larry?"

"The one that called my name right before you stuck me with the needle. The one that said to watch out."

The Doll's shoulders sagged as he exhaled a sigh. "I

suppose it wouldn't hurt to meet your costar before the big scene. Even though I'd wanted it to be a surprise."

"You'll take me to her?"

The Doll looked back over his shoulder. "I'll bring her to you. But you'll have to be ready for her, and in that regard, I have a surprise for you. But you'll need to be hydrated first. We need to make that money shot count."

"Money shot," Larry repeated.

"You know what I mean, Larry. Don't be coy. Oh!" he said brightly. "I nearly forgot. I brought someone to keep you company."

Larry felt his hope rise, though he knew it was foolish. The Doll stepped behind him again, out of sight. Larry turned as far back as he could but couldn't see the man in his peripherals. He turned back to face the screen, his neck strained. He'd learned sometime in his mid-forties than sudden movements were no longer advisable.

A furry, fanged snout entered his field of vision, and he reared back, straining his neck further. The Doll leaped into view, holding a fox mounted on a stand, uttering a high, creepy giggle.

"Oh, I'm sorry, Larry. I just couldn't resist." He turned a key on the fox's flank, gears inside the animal winding. When he set the fox down between Larry and the screen, facing him like a menacing guard dog, the animal's legs began to move on its stand with a sluggish gait while its head swung from side to side, the jaw opening wider and partly closing. "This is Reynard. Reynard is what they call an *automaton*. I know how much you love foxes, though I suppose this wasn't quite what you had in mind."

Again, that high giggle, muffled behind the mask.

"I leave you two to get acquainted," The Doll said, and left the room.

Larry watched the fox as it wound down to a crawl and finally stopped altogether, the light from the projector flickering over its fur and shining in its glassy eyes. Something about it made him think about the drugged woman in the basement. He supposed it was the movement, reminding him of the pistoning dildo, some kind of perpetual motion fucking machine. But that connection didn't feel exactly right, and once he'd noticed, it was impossible to push the thought out of his mind.

8

The Doll returned three sex scenes later with the can of LaCroix. Larry had watched himself cum so many times tonight, he felt like a boxer psyching himself up for a fight by watching his wins over and over again.

I haven't cum like that in a decade, at least. Usually one weak pop and a few dribbles. What's this guy expecting? A load like this? Will he hurt me if I don't cum buckets?

The door opened and The Doll popped the top on the can with a satisfying hiss. Despite his dislike of sparkling water, Larry salivated. The fox watched them as The Doll nursed Larry straight from the can.

"There you go."

The cold liquid bubbled all the way down, with a slight lime taste, moistening every inch of his mouth and tongue and throat. When The Doll removed the can, Larry let out a satisfied gasp.

"Goddamn, that's good. I never liked sparkling water before but I get it now."

"I'm very glad to hear that, Larry. And there's more where that came from. If you cooperate with me, if we trust each other, this doesn't have to end poorly."

"You mean if I play along, I won't get hurt."

The Doll's head tilted, regarding the stuffed animal on the floor. "If you'd prefer," he said.

"Well, I'm ready to play along," Larry told him, just hoping for the chance to get out of this chair. He didn't dare believe this man would let him and Linda go when they were finished the movie. That was giving in to a false sense of security. Best to think the end goal was to kill them both whether they played along or not, and to cooperate until the first opportunity to escape came up.

But he couldn't do that until they were together. Unless he was somehow able to kill The Doll, there was a distinct possibility he'd murder her if Larry escaped on his own, and by the time the cops showed up there would be no evidence left of any of it.

"That's wonderful to hear, Larry. Let's hope your costar feels the same."

9

Larry woke with a start when The Doll came back into the screening room. He hadn't been asleep long, judging by the scene in the film, unless it had already played through again. Maybe twenty minutes, tops. He'd had a nightmare about a menacing shape chasing him through twisting white corridors in the dark. When it finally caught up to him at a dead end, he'd turned to find the shape was a giant sentient version of his own penis, mole and all. The urethra had opened like a mouth and swallowed him whole.

The door opened then, waking him, and for a moment Larry thought his captor had walked away and left the door open, like some kind of test.

After a moment a squeak of metal came from behind the door, followed by another. The door came all the way open, pushed by something on wheels that Larry couldn't quite place at first.

As it neared, with The Doll pushing it, the same wheel squeaking, Larry realized he'd seen this thing before, down in the basement.

It was the gynecology chair. The same woman sat in it, her legs still in the stirrups, still naked beneath the gown. In the light from the projector he saw her cunt clearly. It appeared to be gaping, like her opened mouth, as if it had stuck that way or she was somehow holding it open by sheer force of will.

"Tada!" The Doll said, gesturing toward the chair he'd rolled to a stop directly in front of Larry. The projector image flashed over the woman's pale skin and glassy eyes. She didn't blink.

"What the fuck?" Larry gasped.

It was a doll. Some kind of doctor's manikin.

But what kind of manikin had such realistic features? Why did the skin appear slightly powdered, the lips and eyes glistening with moisture?

"Meet your costar, Mindy St. Pierre."

Larry remembered the name. She'd played the young expectant mother in the doctor scene. The manikin looked somewhat like her, but like a statue in a wax museum it wasn't *quite* the same. It could've passed for a stunt double or a sibling.

"What do you mean, costar?"

"I mean," The Doll said, picking up Reynard the Fox and moving it out of sight, "you're going to fuck her. We've got to get you back in fighting shape before we film the main event."

"I'm not fucking a doll."

"It's never stopped you before. What is it you call the Love Doll you've got tucked away in your closet? Jessica?"

Larry reeled. Nobody knew about Jessica. He hadn't told anyone, not even his closest friends in the business. He hadn't even taken her out of the closet in ages. So how could this freak know about her? Unless he'd been watching Larry long before they first met. Unless he'd been inside Larry's apartment.

"And anyway, Mindy *isn't* a doll. She's a woman."

"Look, I know the difference between a woman and a fucking doll—"

"What I'm telling you, Larry, what you're *failing to grasp* here, is that Mindy St. Pierre isn't a *doll*. She's a real woman. *Was* a real woman. Like Reynard and the animals in my menagerie."

"No," Larry said, the truth of it beginning to sink in.

"Yes." The Doll nodded slowly. "She came here just like you, Larry, looking for a part. She thought she could seduce me into some casting couch nonsense. But she was wrong. *Dead wrong*, you might say." He tittered, that high, creepy laugh Larry had heard when The Doll had shown him the fox. "I drugged her and skinned her alive. Yes, the structure beneath her skin is technically a manikin, and the eyes are glass, but the *rest* of her—the *essence*—is real."

"What the fuck…? What the fucking fuck!"

"Taxidermy is a very *Zen* activity," The Doll said, stroking the dead woman's cheek with the back of a gloved hand. "It's very meticulous. It takes a trained eye and a skilled hand." He returned to Larry, crouching at his knee. "There's something… *sacred*… in knowing you've preserved a thing forever."

The Doll laid a gentle hand on Larry's knee. Larry jerked it away. "You're a fucking psycho."

The Doll shrugged, standing. "Maybe. My point is, if you love something, *lean into it*. Like you did with fucking. You found your niche in a world where most people never discover their purpose, their *raison d'être*, and you *embraced* it, you *made it yours*. Some may have compared you unfavorably in your heyday to court jesters like Ron Jeremy and Harry Reems, but you were a *lion*. King of the Cock." He leaned down, his eyes flickering in the light from the projector. "*Nobody* could fuck like you, Larry. Not Peter North, not John Holmes, not Mandingo. *No one*." He laid both hands on either knee. This time, Larry let him. "You were a *legend*, Larry Walker. You *are* a legend."

The Doll reached behind himself, the hand returning with a pair of clippers. Larry cringed, slamming his knees together to protect his junk.

"Why would I do that?" the freak asked. "I'd no sooner cut off your prick than paint eyebrows on the *Mona Lisa*, or add arms to the *Venus de Milo*."

He opened the blades and slipped them under the zip tie on Larry's left wrist, glancing up to catch Larry's look of anticipation.

"Can I trust you, Larry?"

Larry nodded firmly.

The Doll snipped the zip tie free. Larry raised his hand and wriggled his fingers, loosening the muscles, shaking out the pins and needles.

The Doll scooched over and snipped the tie on his right hand. With two hands free he could choke the man if he wanted to. But what good would it do? His ankles were still tied, the leather strap was still tight around his chest. He could kill the man and still end up stuck here, starving to death while his most famous film played on an endless loop, driving him to insanity.

He massaged his wrists while The Doll snipped the ties on his ankles. Then Larry twisted and rolled his feet. With all the pain in his wrists he'd barely noticed how bad off his feet were.

"I'm going to let you out of the chair now. If you try anything..."

"I won't."

"Good. Because I won't harm your face, Larry. Or your genitals. But there are things I can do, *techniques* I've learned, that would make emasculation feel like a day at the spa. You do not want to test me."

Larry nodded.

The Doll nodded in response. "Good," he said, then moved behind Larry. The sound of chains rattling, and a padlock being opened. Then, suddenly, the pressure on Larry's chest loosened.

He grabbed the back of the chair and pushed himself to his feet. He staggered, walked a few steps. The Doll continued messing with the chains behind him, making a racket. How many hours had he been strapped to that chair? What day was it? He stretched his arms. The dead woman stared at him. He stayed as far away from her as he could.

"That's better, isn't it?"

The door was still open. He could run right now if he wanted to. But Linda was somewhere in the basement. If he ran, she would die.

What if it's not her? What if that was a trick? The whole thing felt like a setup, didn't it? Just go, *man. Make a fuckin run for it.*

He took two steps to the side, testing the limits of his freedom. With two further, more confident steps something yanked back jarringly, causing him to stagger backward and almost lose his balance.

He caught the back of the chair and peered behind it, not understanding what had happened. Now it made sense. He wasn't free. The strap around his chest was connected to a length of chain that ran through a hole in the back of the chair. The chain ended at a metal loop bolted to the cement floor.

The Doll watched him from behind the mask. "I hope you weren't planning to walk away."

Larry shook his head.

"That's good, Larry. I've given you enough chain to do what I've asked. Please don't use it to hang yourself."

Larry regarded the dead woman. Aside from having once been a live human being, how much different was she from Jessica the Love Doll?

"I can't."

"You *will.*"

He shook his head, his body beginning to tremble uncontrollably. "Why? Just... just tell me why."

"Why is not your concern. You're an actor. *Act.*"

He shook his head again. The woman stared at him, her glassy eyes judging him.

"Larry. *Larry.*"

Larry looked up at The Doll.

"How many women have you treated like objects? How is this any different?"

"It *is* different!"

"*Why?*"

"Because I'm not a fucking necrophiliac, you psycho! She was a fucking living *human being*! All she wanted was a role in a goddamn movie, just like me, and for that you *skin her alive*? Make her into a fucking sex doll? What kind of sick-fuck logic is that, huh? Why do you wear that fucking mask? *What the fuck fucked you up in the head so bad?*"

The Doll stared at him for a long moment. The woman stared at him. Finally, the Doll blinked.

"This isn't going to be a confessional, Larry. Either you fuck Mindy, or the two of you switch places in the stirrups and I wheel in her robot friend. I could leave you to its mercy for days. How long do you think you'd last before you develop the first fissure? How long until you pass out from the pain, or internal bleeding?"

"*Fine.*"

The Doll cocked his head. "Beg pardon?"

"*I said I'll fucking do it.*"

"Well, that's very good to hear, Larry. I'm glad you've decided to come around." The Doll approached the woman in the chair, reached for something beside her and held it out to him.

Larry regarded the bottle of oil-based lube for a long moment. He still wasn't sure he could go through with this—the dead woman would be staring at him the entire time with her glassy eyes. But he snatched the bottle from The Doll's gloved hand and reached for his zipper.

This was a line he'd never even *considered* crossing, forced or otherwise. Of course there were half a dozen dark tales of snuff sex tapes passing around the industry, but no one he knew had ever seen a *real* one. They were rumors. Things to frighten the newbies.

Now here he was about to *star* in one.

If this ever got out… if this ever hit the public…

But it wouldn't. That wasn't what The Doll was about. This was meant to be private. He'd called it a "shrine." He'd never be able to show it to anyone because then his secret life would be revealed.

It was cold comfort. It still meant Larry had to fuck a corpse.

He pulled his cock out through the y-front of his underwear. He swallowed hard, closed his eyes, licked his dry lips, and began tugging on his foreskin.

I can do this.

"Open your eyes, Larry."

He did. The Doll held a high-end prosumer video camera to his left eye, pointed at Larry's face.

"Fuck her like you mean it. The camera wants to see that famous Walker passion in your eyes."

Larry gazed over the top of her head, unfocused on the film, not daring to meet those glassy eyes, and got himself hard.

"Touch her, Larry. She's ready for you."

It's skin. Real human skin.

He reached out and touched her stomach, surprisingly smooth and firm yet yielding, like touching a pillow made of lambskin.

I can do this.

He grasped her hip, smooth, firm, the feel bone under the skin. Or an armature, he supposed. His fingers pressed into it, making slight creaking sounds, like easing into a leather couch. The effect was nearly enough to make him lose his erection.

You've fucked in front of a thousand strangers. You've cum in high-heel shoes and peanut butter jars and potted plants. Pretend it's a doll and fuck it, you coward.

He tried pushing the head of his cock into her open hole, but it stuck against the sides.

The lube.

He reached behind himself, still jerking off, not

wanting to lose this rod. His fingers touched the bottle and he grasped it, brought it over and drizzled some onto his prick. He worked it over the head and down the shaft, reaching back and placing the bottle back on the chair.

"*Good*," The Doll said.

Okay. Here goes…

He pushed into the leathery hole. This time, with his cock sufficiently lubed, it slid in not quite easily, due to the width of the hole, but with a grip that felt *almost* real. He supposed if he turned a lambskin glove inside out and filled it with lube, fucking it would feel something like this, which—if he pushed away the thought that it was human leather, that those glassy eyes weren't real but the teeth and hair and fingernails probably were—he had to admit felt almost… *good*.

Instinctually, his eyes fell over the dead woman's body, moving quickly past her perpetually staring eyes to her glossy, half-parted lips—the tongue inside, probably fake, moist and touching the backs of her upper teeth—her long, smooth neck, her perky tits which would never sag with small puffy nipples, her belly a smooth slight paunch, her cunt plucked hairless, the folds rosy pink as he plunged in and out. The Doll must have measured the length of it perfectly because when balls deep, the head of his prick hit its rounded end, like pounding against a cervix.

Larry thrust and thrust, getting into it, doing his job, playing the role, and The Doll shot the scene from various angles. He had to admit she had a passing resemblance to the woman on the screen. But she *wasn't* her. Larry had seen Mindy St. Pierre at the AVNs in the early 2000s. After a few DUIs and a brief stint in rehab she'd gained about a hundred pounds. She'd looked healthy but *nothing* like she did back then.

This dead woman was somebody's daughter, someone's sister. A Missing Person. Gone to an audition at some empty office park in Encino or Culver City and never heard from again. Yet another wannabe starlet used and abused by this heartless city and left a literal empty shell, a shell stuffed with sawdust and doll armature and, currently, Larry's rock-hard, lubed-up eleven-inch cock.

Despite these thoughts and the uncanny valley quality to her face and skin and the inhuman texture of her vagina, Larry felt a tingle in his balls signifying his imminent climax. He reached out and grabbed the dead woman's hair. The soft, silky texture—far more human than the rest of her—pushed him over the edge and he came hard, filling her hole, shooting gouts onto her stomach, into her belly button. The force of his cum was so powerful his whole body seemed to deflate, and he fell over her chest, breathing heavily.

An incessant buzz filled the room, so loud Larry at first thought he'd been struck by lightning, some kind of moral punishment for ejaculating on a dead woman's corpse. Fistfuls of her hair came away from her head, twisted through his fingers. He shook them away in disgust and got to his feet, panting, his erection wilting.

The Doll lowered the camera from his eye and craned his neck toward the plain white ceiling.

"*Fuck*," he muttered. "Stay put. I've got to get the door."

With that, he crossed the room, leaving Larry alone with the lube and the cum-drenched dead woman and his film—currently the "Mrs. S. Fucks the Milkman" scene—playing on an endless loop. He waited to hear the sound of the latches and locks, but there was nothing beyond the click of the door as The Doll pulled it shut.

The door was unlocked.

Larry tucked his sticky, wilted cock back in his jeans and hurried back to where the chain met the link on the floor. He grabbed it close to the base and pulled as hard as he could, gaining nothing but a strained shoulder.

"Okay, *think*, Larry, fucking *think*."

The chain looped from the floor through a hole in the back of the chair. He'd never actually been strapped to the chair itself, only pulled so taut against it that it felt like he'd been strapped securely to the chair. There was a good... maybe five feet of slack sagging between the chair and the floor. He could reach the giant projector looping cabinet from here, if not for the chair. Turn off that fucking film.

But what if he did, and The Doll came back before he'd gotten free? What then? He'd already made him fuck a corpse, and even though he didn't technically *enjoy* it, he *did* ejaculate. What worse could he possibly do to him?

You want worse, he already promised it.

He'd strap Larry to the *other* chair, that was worse. He'd use her pistoning dildo friend Robocock on Larry's poor hemorrhoidic pucker until he passed out or died.

So... what then? Keep pulling on the chain? Pray to God he could break free?

Someone's at the door, right? Should I scream? Would they hear me?

He shook his head.

Nah. If nobody heard his other victims, they wouldn't hear me. The house is concrete. The basement's probably got better soundproofing than a Melrose recording studio.

"You gotta do *something*, man, don't just stand here like a prick."

He looked around the room. The dead woman. The chair, bolted to the floor. The projector cabinet. The lube.

"*The lube.*"

He hurried back to the chair and grabbed the bottle, turned it around and read the instructions. DO NOT INGEST. DO NOT USE NEAR EYES OR MOUTH.

Larry briefly wondered how many quarts of personal lubricant he'd swallowed in his lifetime. Then he gathered up the slack of the chain, making sure it was easily accessible on the far side of the chair, where he stood awaiting The Doll's return.

He stood poised with the lube in his right hand, only realizing he was gripping it too hard when he noticed his hand shaking. He steadied his hand, did a bit of meditative breathing. In through the nose, out through the mouth.

The door finally unlatched.

Could he do it? Would he chicken out?

What if nothing happened? What if he got the lube in The Doll's eyes and it didn't do anything? What if he squirted the entire bottle at the freak and it missed the eyeholes of that fucking mask?

The door swung open. The Doll stepped in.

"Fucking lawyers," he said with a dramatic sigh. "Am I right? Now, where were—"

The moment The Doll came within spitting distance, Larry snapped open the bottle with his thumb and squirted it squarely between the eyeholes on the mask.

The Doll cried out, grasping at his face.

Larry grabbed the length of chain and ran at him. He swung it over the freak's shoulders once, twice, and pulled.

The Doll grabbed at him, clawing and screeching, eyes red and raw through the eyeholes. Larry held fast, ignoring the freak's manicured nails digging into his throat, bringing blood. He'd kill the fucker even if it was the last thing he'd do. Just hope to God he had the keys on him somewhere.

The Doll grabbed him by the shoulders and launched

the two of them into the gynecology chair. The dead woman toppled, sprawling on the floor in the same seated, spreadeagle position, like a statue made of human leather. Larry noticed neat lines of stitching up the backs of her arms and legs and along the spine as his jism oozed from her perpetually open hole onto the floor.

He slammed The Doll against the chair, pressing his face into the hard, mint-green Naugahyde, choking harder. The man gagged. The mask came off as they struggled and Larry startled at the face he'd revealed.

Though his hair was a sweaty mess and his eyes were raw, streaming tears, behind the mask was the same man who'd let Larry in the night of the audition, well dressed, with the slight British accent. It was Jason's "butler," Reed.

"What the fuck...?"

Reed or Jason or whoever the fuck he was reached down. At first, Larry thought he was reaching for his junk and he took a single step back. Then the hand shot up, and he felt a sting in his midsection. He looked down just as the freak depressed the plunger, filling him with whatever he'd shot him up with that first night, though likely at a higher dose this time.

Larry squeezed, pulling the chains as hard as he could. The Doll gasped and choked and his red-raw eyes were beginning to dilate, but his lips upturned in a smile, his teeth pink with blood. Larry was losing his fight against the drug coursing through his system. Either one of them would survive, or they would die together. The freak seemed to be betting on himself, or neither.

Larry's arms grew numb. He pulled with every last bit of strength. How long did it take to choke a man to death? How long until his arms became so numb he could no longer hold the chain?

His vision began to gray, slipping away at the sides. The last thing he saw before passing out was his captor's blood-pinked smile, and the flicker of the film in his insane eyes.

10

Awakened from another dreamless sleep, Larry discovered himself restrained and sitting again, only this time he appeared to be moving.

He heard the squeak and rumble of wheels beneath him. Smooth white walls stood on either side of the conveyance, whatever it was. For the moment, his head seemed to be as immobile as the rest of him. The occasional inset bulb illuminated the corridor from the equally white ceiling.

Were these the halls he'd run through the other night, trying to escape after The Doll had hit him with the drug the first time? No wonder he'd had difficulty. They took one corner after another, as if heading deeper and deeper into a labyrinth.

Finally, they entered a large, dark room with a very high ceiling.

"Oh, you're awake," The Doll said. The sound of a switch being thrown was followed by dozens of track lights coming to life twenty feet above Larry's head. He squinted against the brightness.

"Where are you taking me?"

"I'm afraid this is your final stop, Larry. The end of the line. You really shouldn't have tried to hurt me."

The freak leaned over him. Behind the mask, his eyes were clear and no longer red. But the marks on his stubbled throat would be impossible to ignore. Someone would ask questions. Maybe someone who was already curious about Jason Reed's private life.

Larry giggled.

"What are you laughing at?" came The Doll's muffled response.

"You, you fucking psycho *freak*," Larry said, through his laughter. "Why the fuck are you still wearing that thing, huh? I've already seen your face."

"But your costar hasn't."

"Is she here? *Linda!*" he called out. "*LINDA!*"

"Linda is sleeping right now."

"I want to see her."

"You've got no right to make demands."

"I'm the *star*, goddammit! I fucked your Frankenstein, now fucking let me see *Linda*!"

The Doll stopped rolling him forward. After a moment, he said, "Very well." Then he rolled Larry forward again, stopped a moment later and turned him around. "Here she is. You see? She's sleeping."

Larry managed to lower his head, resting his chin in his jugular notch. The scene displayed before him, set inside another glassed-in cement box, looked exactly like Mr. and Mrs. S's bedroom from the film, down to the pea-yellow color of their sheets and the black and white photographs on the night stands. The amount of detail the freak had gone to, whether himself or some interior decorator, unaware of their intent, possibly believing them to be some sort of art installation, was incredible. Like the doctor's office, it looked like a scene pulled straight out of the 1970s, like a strange cubed time capsule.

Linda Flint lay on the bed, her curly blonde hair pulled up, dressed in a silky nightgown. Her chest, which she'd never gotten augmented, even when most women with small breasts in the industry were doing it, rose and fell beneath the retro flower-print duvet.

He called out her name again. Her eyelids didn't flutter. She didn't even stir under the covers.

"I told you, she's sleeping. She's been very busy."

"She's okay? You haven't hurt her?"

"Does it look like she's been hurt?"

She looked fine. She looked like an angel.

It hurt to see her trapped in a box, like The Doll's other women—at least he assumed there were others. There were five more cement cubes down here, each likely containing its own scene from the film. Each with its own manikin made from human skin.

The chair began rolling slowly down the corridor between the cubes. Larry examined the first as they passed, slow enough to see that while The Doll hadn't been in the screening room with him, he'd been busy down here filming Linda's "scenes." On TV screens set up on either side of this tableau the original scene played in-sync with a newly filmed version, in which Linda blew and rode the quarterback reverse cowgirl. Within the locker room set, a young man lay across the bench in football gear, his arms raised to remove his helmet from his shaggy hippy hair. His bare chest, lean arms and face had the same leathery, not-quite-human look as Mindy St. Pierre's, his glassy eyes looking down as the large erection protruding upward from his knickerbockers, where Linda would've been during the filming.

In the scene on the left screen, filmed during the '70s, Linda's enthusiasm was infectious. She'd been one of the best in the business. Colleagues called her "Eveready," after the battery, because she'd had the uncanny ability to get wet without any physical stimulation, like a dramatic actor able to cry on command. She'd been the female equivalent of a woodsman, a perfect pairing for Larry.

In the scene on the right, Linda was clearly disturbed. She gorged on the leathery member, cradling the dead man's hairless balls, as a single tear spilled from her one visible eye.

"Why are you doing this to us?"

The Doll slowly turned the chair, and began rolling him toward their destination. "I suppose I owe you *some* sort of explanation, don't I? After all, you are my muse, Larry. Do you know the story of Pygmalion?"

"Yeah, the uh… isn't that what they based *Opening of Misty Beethoven* on? 'The rain in Spain stays on the plain' and shit?"

"Not the play. The figure from Greek mythology."

Larry shook his head. "Never heard of him."

"Well, Larry, in Ovid's *Metamorphosis*, Pygmalion was a sculptor so disgusted by prostitution he became celibate, choosing instead to spend his time with a woman he'd carved from ivory. He named her Galetea. He became so enamored by Galatea he began kissing and fondling her, and eventually fell in love with his own creation.

"One day, the day of Venus's festival, Pygmalion made a wish that he would find a woman who was the living embodiment of Galatea. When he arrived home, he kissed his ivory lover and discovered her lips were warm. Her breast warms and softens to his touch 'as wax grows soft in sunshine.'"

"Then what happens?"

"Then she wakes and they have a daughter together. It's a very brief and unsatisfying conclusion."

"So, what? You get in the boxes and fuck these things?"

"Don't be distasteful."

"Then what? Give me *something*. You said this is a shrine to me, you said I'm your muse, don't you *want* to tell me?"

"That's not entirely true. It is a shrine to you, but not *just* to you. When I was a young boy, maybe eight or nine, I fell in love with a picture in a magazine. I found it in the woods, in what looked like a hobo's encampment.

"The story that went along with the pictures called her Denise. She had curly blonde hair in a high ponytail and wore workout clothes from the era, which was the 1980s: a red one-piece bikini with blue leggings and white sneakers and a yellow sweatband. When I got a little older some boys and I managed to sneak into the adult section of the video store. It wasn't too difficult. Someone distracts the clerks while another plays lookout, and the rest sneak through the curtain. I searched and searched for my Denise among all the videotapes, and when I finally came across one that looked something like her it turned out to be a different woman altogether. Her name was Amber Lynn. But I still couldn't find Denise. I later discovered her name wasn't Denise at all. It was Linda Flint."

As he said this, he rolled Larry to a stop in front of another diorama. This one contained the kitchen set for the Milkman scene. The milkman himself stood against the kitchen island. Bottles of milk lay spilled on the floor around his feet. On the screens, Linda took the Milkman's hot load on her tits, already glistening with the milk she'd poured down them. In the original, Linda laughed as the Milkman covers her face and tits, smearing it all over herself and rubbing the glistening head of his cock on her face. In The Doll's version, Linda startled as a geyser erupted from the dead man's prick. It looked as though she wasn't expecting the thing to actually ejaculate. The stream of pearlescent fluid struck her eyes, down her throat—she gagged—and basted her breasts, heavier than they'd been during her porn career, plumped from two pregnancies and the baby weight she'd never managed to fully lose.

Linda reacted to something off camera—verbal cues from The Doll, most likely—then forced a smile as another spurt of fake sperm splashed her forehead.

Larry felt himself stiffening again, despite whatever drugs The Doll had pumped into him, what he'd just been forced to do with the dead woman, and what Linda had been subjected to in the film. It was an animal reaction. He could no more prevent it than stop his heart from beating. The scene disgusted him, but disgust had rarely prevented him from getting hard in the past. Call it the Curse of the Woodsman.

"From then on," The Doll said while the scene looped back to the beginning, "I began ordering pornographic films through the mail, pretending to be the owner of a video rental house. The tapes always came in large boxes filled otherwise with mainstream theatrical releases. I told my parents I was studying them so I could be a director. They were likely just pleased I was no longer interested in creating automatons and *tableau vivant* from dead animals. I believe they found that hobby *strange*."

As the Doll continued his story, he moved the chair onward, passing a bedroom set that Larry didn't recognize. Though it looked like the same era as the film, it was much more extravagant. The two screens in the high corners were turned off, their screens black.

"While I amassed my film library in an east-wing room my father soon designated my screening room, for which he bought a projector and screen and all sorts of state-of-the-art equipment to encourage what they saw as a 'safe' hobby, I kept my *secret* collection in a hole in the wall of my walk-in closet. When my parents left for whatever it was they did together on the weekends, play tennis or lunch at the club, I brought one or two tapes to the screening room, locked the door so Reed, our butler, wouldn't walk in on me, and watched the tapes with the sound turned off."

Larry absorbed the fact that The Doll's butler's name was Reed and clearly couldn't have been his own, but didn't acknowledge it. "Didn't he have a key?"

"My parents made sure the staff weren't to disturb me while I was 'studying.' And anyway, I was too young to masturbate. They would only have caught me watching the films with the rapturous attentiveness of a young acolyte hearing the Gospel. I *was* studying, you see, but not to be a director. I wanted to be a *star*."

"It's not all it's cracked up to be, believe me."

"But you got to fuck Linda Flint *in her prime*. Kay Parker, Jeanna Fine, Bambi Woods, on and on—"

"It's a job." Larry managed a shrug. "I also fucked a lot of ditch pigs."

"Larry, I'm aware the adult industry isn't everything a pubescent boy imagines it would be. I've also had my share of porn stars. Big names. Their tapes are in my library, if you don't believe me. But it's not about the *act*, Larry, it's about the *fantasy*."

He stopped the chair again just close enough for Larry to see the gynecologist's office set in one of the last two cubes. The cube to the left of it was dark. It was impossible to see through its glass, only the reflection of the other cubes and the two of them standing between them on its surface.

"When I discovered *The Awakening of Mr. and Mrs. S*, it was *my own* awakening. My parents were heading toward a divorce at the time. Even the staff were talking about it, in hushed tones, when they thought no one was listening. But I was listening, Larry. I loved my parents, as much as I was able, despite not having very much to do with them. I knew something had to be done.

"Do you remember the film *The Parent Trap*? Not the sequels or the subpar remake. I mean the original 1961 film with Haley Mills playing the twins."

Larry remembered it. The film had come out when he was eight or nine. He'd seen it with his mother and little brother in the theater. His mother, who'd recently gone through a very ugly divorce after catching his father "in the act" with another woman, had been very vocal about the film after they'd left the theater. If they hadn't lived on a fixed income she likely would've made them leave halfway through.

"It's important to bear in mind that I was quite young and naïve at the time I came up with my plan to prevent my parents from getting a divorce. I based it on Mr. S's scheme to trigger his wife's sexuality in *Awakening*. I paid to place an ad in the classifieds of a local newspaper known for its risqué back pages. In it, I asked for a man looking for a discreet encounter, no names and no strings attached. They were to call the number I provided, which was to the payphone across the street from where I grew up.

"I figured it would receive a handful of calls at most. You wouldn't believe how many men called that payphone, Larry. Day and night for days. Or perhaps you would. Suffice to say, I found who I imagined would be the right fit quickly, and canceled the ad the same day. I pitched my voice up high to sound like a woman, which wasn't too much higher than my voice at the time, since I was young enough that it hadn't changed yet."

"Wait a minute," Larry said, trying to look over his shoulder at the freak in the mask. "I remember reading about this in the late '80s. That kid was *you*?"

"It's rude to skip ahead, Larry. Fortunately, most people don't remember the story. It was a blip, coming as it did during the heat of the Menendez trial. But I'll never forget, Larry. As I'm sure you can imagine.

"I was home when it happened. I told the man—I never got his name but I discovered it later, after everything was said and done—I told him to enter through the back door. I said—using what I thought was a sultry female voice—that I'd leave it open. That I'd be horny and waiting for him. He was to go upstairs and ravage me, and not to take no for an answer: just like Mr. S told the Milkman. I knew my mother would be loaded up on so much Valium she'd have passed out in front of *All My Children*—"

"And you thought she'd be fine with some guy breaking into her house and *raping* her?"

The Doll stepped out in front of him, staring down through the eyeholes of the mask. "My only awareness of sex was from pornography, Larry. How could I know what you did was wrong? It worked out well for Mr. and Mrs. S, didn't it?"

"You're blaming Linda and me for some movie we made for a few thousand bucks forty years ago! That's what this is all about? That's why you kidnapped us? Forced me to… to fuck that *thing*?"

The Doll didn't respond, merely continued with his tale. "The man entered our house through the back door at three-thirty-seven pm," he said. "Police found no sign of a break in, of course. From the back door, the man entered the kitchen. He opened the fridge, took one of my father's imported beers and drank it on the way upstairs. The police found the bottle cap discarded on the kitchen floor.

"As expected, the man found my mother passed out in bed. He entered the room and turned off the television. He took off his clothes while he approached her."

"Is this from the police report?" Larry asked. The level of detail had to either be from the report or imagined.

"I set up cameras, Larry. Remember? I was studying to be a director, or so my parents thought. I had cameras in the kitchen, the foyer, the master bedroom. He was fully undressed before reaching my mother in the bed. He was masturbating."

"*Jesus*, dude. It's your mother."

"The police never discovered my tapes. In fact, I still have them. I watched them, afterwards. I had to know what happened. I had to know *why* and *how*. My mother woke up with him on top of her. He'd already climbed under the duvet and was fondling one of her breasts, like Pygmalion and his Galatea. Only my mother didn't warm to his touch. What she did was *scream*. He forced his lips over hers and she continued screaming into his open mouth. I heard her from the screening room in the east wing. I was terrified. I'd never heard my mother scream like that before. Or after.

"Why didn't you help her?"

"I was twelve years old, Larry. Alone in a palatial estate filled with valuable items and a safe full of cash. I'd sent Reed out on an errand. It was just my mother and me in the house. And the man, of course. The man I'd told not to take no for an answer. The man who likely wondered how he'd gotten so lucky to stumble into some lonely housewife's rape fantasy. No names. No strings.

"It was several minutes later according to the timecode on the tapes, when my father returned home early from a business meeting, though in my mind it felt like *hours*, sitting alone in my screening room, waiting for it all to be over, while my mother was being raped. I saw him arrive on the tape from the foyer camera after the police left. He heard noises from upstairs. The moans and grunts of a man and a woman. He retrieved his gun from the table in the foyer, a snubnosed .38-calibre Detective Special, and crept up the stairs.

"He found the man and my mother in bed together. I can only imagine what he must have thought, because he didn't hesitate. He shot the man in the head. His entire face exploded over my mother, showering her with blood and teeth and brains, and when she managed to push the dead man off of her, my father shot at her three times. The camera in the bedroom didn't catch his expression, only the back of his head as he determined what must have been happening there that afternoon. The first two shots missed. Feathers burst from the pillows. The camera did capture my mother's look of fear turning to hope as she reached out to her husband, my father, readying to plead for her life. Her mouth had barely opened before the third shot struck her in the chest, puncturing her heart. She died almost instantly.

"My father approached the bed. He stood over his dead wife and what he imagined must be her lover, the man who'd been slowly pushing her away from him for almost a year, edging them closer and closer toward divorce. With his face half turned toward the camera, it did capture his look of resolve as he put the pistol to his own forehead and pulled the trigger. The gun fell from his hand and his body collapsed over my mother and the man in the bed. The rest you already know, since you read about it in the paper."

"Jesus fuck, man," Larry said. "Look, I'm sorry that happened. But that's not our fault. It's *nobody's* fault. You didn't understand what you were doing and we just made a fun little skin flick. I mean, who the hell could imagine some kid would copy that scene? What are the odds?"

"I don't know the odds, Larry. What I do know is that my final tableau requires a happy couple."

"You're gonna kill us, aren't you? Skin us alive. Make us into one of them?"

The Doll tilted his head against his shoulder in what Larry thought looked like sympathy. "Oh, Larry, I would never hurt you. At least not like that. You were my TV father. Other boys had Steven Keaton or Danny Tanner or Uncle Phil. I had you. And Linda was my TV mother."

Larry considered mentioning how warped that was, that two actors who'd worked in a few skin flicks together would be surrogates for anyone's parents. But he was pretty sure The Doll already knew it.

"I just need the two of you to work together one last time. Let me preserve it with my cameras. And then I'll set you free, I promise you."

"Both of us?"

"Both of you. You'll be happy to know your costar has already consented."

Larry didn't believe him, but it wasn't as if he could do anything to prevent whatever came next. He'd already tried to escape and been caught, tried to kill his captor and failed. What else could he do but play along and hope the two of them together might be able to overpower the freak or convince him to let them go?

He looked at his reflection in the dark surface of the glass in the final cube. He looked for a long time. The years had taken their toll. The booze and drugs hadn't been kind. What if he could relive that Golden Age of youth, right here in The Doll's basement? Larry and Linda together again. Not on the screen, but in reality. Not exactly consensual, but on a level playing field of coercion.

How many times had he imagined being with her again, the way they were then, while he watched their scenes and jerked himself to climax? Her smell. Her taste. Her eyes and smile and every inch of her body.

"Okay," he said finally.

The Doll nodded. "I'm very glad to hear that, Larry. One last shot and you'll be free. After everything I've put the two of you through to prepare you for your Big Scene, isn't it wonderful to know you'll be freeing each other?"

11

The Doll wheeled Larry back to the screening room with no punishment for attempting to murder him, despite the prominent bruises from the chain visible on his stubbly neck. Larry supposed the freak was feeling generous, that the implication of violent penetration the gynecologist chair threatened had only been to facilitate his compliance in the "Big Scene," which he imagined would take place in the final cube.

Whatever the reason, The Doll whistled a cheery tune as he rolled Larry back to the white room. Larry didn't recognize the song until he was secured again to the chair bolted to the floor, and the freak was hefting the dead woman—Larry's sperm dripping from her hole—back onto the gynecologist chair.

It was the theme song from *The Parent Trap*.

He popped the top off another La Croix and offered it to Larry. Larry nodded, his thirst almost overpowering. The Doll nursed him. Larry guzzled the fizzy liquid, feeling it hydrating every crevasse of his body.

"I'll be back soon," The Doll said, a smile in his voice as he returned to the dead woman in the chair. "Take five, as they say. Do whatever you need to prepare. You'll be in front of the camera again very soon, Larry. The climactic return of Larry Walker to the pornographic film industry!" He shook his head in awe. "You can't *begin* to imagine how excited I feel right now...."

Uttering his high-pitched giggle, he rolled the chair toward the door.

"'Prepare,'" Larry muttered to himself once the man had left. He raised his hands the half inch they would move from the armrests, held with zip ties. "Yeah, how the fuck am I supposed to do that?"

Even if his hands hadn't been zip-tied to the chair, the current scene playing on the wall, in which a young Linda Flint was ravaged by a man credited as The Milkman, no longer aroused him. It was doubly tainted, by the horrors Linda had been subjected to in the cube room, and the terrible secret The Doll had revealed about his shattered childhood.

If by some miracle he made it out of here alive, Larry doubted he'd ever be able to jerk off to this film ever again. A small price to pay, he supposed, for the trauma it had put the three of them through.

"Now what?" he said aloud.

He glanced to the left of him, startling at the sight of Reynard the automaton. He'd forgotten The Doll had moved it out of the way when he'd wheeled in the dead woman. It stared up at him with its mouth half open, baring teeth in a wolfish smile.

"Shut up," he told it.

The fox continued smiling.

Several minutes later, once the Milkman had emptied

his balls on Linda's face and chest and the next dialogue scene began in Larry's office, The Doll returned. He carried with him a set of clothing draped over one forearm and a packet of boner pills.

"I wasn't sure if you'd need these but I brought them just in case," he said, approaching the chair. "I know in your interview with Luke Ford you said you quit acting in porn because of what the pills did to you, then I figured one last time couldn't hurt, right? I'm going to untie you so you can change into your costume. You'll be good, won't you?"

Larry nodded.

The Doll nodded back. He began by snipping the zip ties, like before, then undid the chained strap from around Larry's chest. Larry stood and took the neatly folded pile of clothes when The Doll offered them.

"I never wore these in the movie," he said, looking at the faded denim jeans, a pair of tighty-whities—a rare item in porn—white tube socks and a Def Leppard T-shirt with the sleeves cut off.

"No," The Doll said. "You didn't."

Larry frowned, not getting it. This was supposed to be the recreation of a scene from *The Awakening of Mr. and Mrs. S*, wasn't it? Why would he make him wear something that wasn't from the movie?

"Put them on, please."

Larry undressed, glad to be out of his soiled clothes and to put on something fresh, whether it was from the film or not. "I guess it's too much to ask for a shower?"

"No need." The freak produced a small, long-necked green bottle from the right front pocket of his slacks.

"Brut for Men," Larry said, reading the label. "There's a throwback."

"Yes," The Doll said. He spritzed some at Larry's

armpits and groin as Larry pulled up the fresh underpants. It permeated Larry's nostrils, a spicy woodsy scent with an undercurrent of citrus. Better than his current musky funk, he supposed.

"Better spritz the b-hole to be safe," he said, turning and slipping the underwear partway down. A light hiss was followed by a cool misting on his ass cheeks and pucker. He tugged the underwear back up, then pulled on the socks one by one.

When he was fully dressed he felt ridiculous. He hadn't worn a muscle tee in decades, and the wrinkled skin hanging from his pallid biceps didn't quite fit the style. He shrugged. "How do I look?"

"Almost perfect," The Doll said. He stepped forward and pressed something over Larry's upper lip. It felt sticky and tickled his nose.

"Is that a fake mustache?"

"It is," The Doll said.

"I didn't have a mustache."

"No. You didn't. Are you ready for your Big Reunion?"

Larry was. Aside from just a little while ago in the cube, he hadn't seen Linda in a few years. She'd always been busy with one of her husband's films, and when they did get together Chet was always there, like a chaperone. Though he claimed to be "cool," Larry had always figured Chet Daniels was a little jealous of their friendship. The kid was in his thirties. He hadn't even been a gleam in his father's eye when Larry and Linda had acted in their first scene together.

"Let's go meet your Leading Lady," The Doll said, ushering him forward.

Larry had never left the room without being under the effects of the drugs. On the way back from the cube room he'd been lying down, strapped to the gynecologist chair. He hadn't seen that the winding stairs stood right across the corridor from the door to the screening room, but from what he remembered of his first time down here, it made sense. The cube room stood a short distance to their right, the room fully lit.

The Doll led him forward. He felt like a groom walking up the aisle with his father. But where was the bride?

The cube to their left, the doctor's scene, was set up as it had been when he'd first come down here, with the piston pumping the dildo in and out of Mindy St. Pierre's leathery vagina. The one to their right remained unlit. He paused a moment to look at himself in the dark glass. He looked strange. He hadn't worn a mustache or a cut-off tee since the late-'80s. The only thing missing was his sweet mullet.

"What's in that box?"

"Would you like to see the tableau, Larry?"

Larry looked at his reflection. The Doll standing next to him, his head tilted quizzically to the side. He nodded.

The Doll draped an arm over his shoulders. "Very well. But you know what they say, Larry: curiosity killed the cat. Are you sure you want to see?"

What could possibly be inside? From what he'd seen of the other cubes, the last scene of the movie was the only one missing: the orgy at the neighbor's house, played by Mike Horner and Annette Haven, set in a sunken living room like the one in Larry's apartment, with shag carpet, a disco ball and lava lamps, the stereotypical swingers' pad from the '70s.

Could it really be that bad?

Considering what the others had inside? Yeah, he thought. *Pretty sure it's gonna be bad. Are you sure you wanna see this?*

He nodded again.

"All right," The Doll said. He removed his arm from Larry's shoulders and approached the box. "Now, Larry, I want you to understand that what you'll see inside is my masterwork. Everything I've done in my entire life led to this creation."

"Just turn on the fucking light."

The Doll chuckled once, then pressed a button on the side of the cube and stepped aside.

Larry's anxious reflection vanished from the glass as the inside of the cube illuminated. If it hadn't he would've seen his expression shift from apprehension to realization to panicked terror in a single blink. He stepped back in horror, bile rising in his throat as the scene within the cube came to life.

As he'd expected the set was a prefect replica of Horner and Haven's living room, only what was on the set he could never have imagined. Mounted on the floor, on the sofa, on the La-Z-Boy recliner and propped up on throw pillows, six men and six women flayed alive by The Doll, their cured flesh stretched over animatronic armatures and pillow stuffing, writhed, grinded, humped and thrust their crotches into the dead-eyed faces of their partners. The eyes, susceptible to decay, replaced with prosthetics, glassy and unblinking. Their open mouths, tongues protruding in orgiastic ecstasy, made of plastic or plaster glued to the inside of the skulls. Their gears and pulleys whined and buzzed as their leathery bodies moved without rhythm, permanently erect members plunging into always wet, always open mouths and vaginas, fingers stroking back and forth like clockwork cuckoos, hands jerking up and down mechanically. From the speaker came the moans and grunts of the film's soundtrack, playing on the TV monitor at the far left of the cube. The monitor on the right remained blank.

Buzzzzz—click-click-click and a cock entered an open mouth to slurps and moans from the film.

Whirrrrr—chug-chug-chug and a dead woman's head descended jerkily between another dead woman's legs. The lips smacked on the soundtrack as the automaton simulated cunnilingus.

Despite the horribly unhuman quality to the movement, Larry found he couldn't pry his gaze away. It was repulsive yet fascinating. The more he looked the more details he noticed: the stitching under a breast, at the backs of the arms and along the spine like the dead woman he'd been forced to fuck in the white room. The fake facial hair and pubic wigs glued to their desiccated skin to recreate the era and actors whose roles they were playing. The cracks and aging in their skin like old leather, some much more noticeable than others. Early kills, Larry assumed, several of which were sewn up with thicker thread, leaking bits of stuffing. He was certain he recognized at least a few faces from auditions, though none of them were actors from the original scene. The blonde between another woman's legs looked almost exactly like the woman behind the desk at the empty office, and though the skin itself looked fresh enough, he couldn't get a good enough look to be sure with her head bobbing jerkily up and down.

"Fuck…" he croaked. "What the fucking fuck?"

"Does that mean you like it?"

"Turn it off. *Turn it the fuck off!*"

The Doll flicked off the switch. Immediately the cube darkened and the film's soundtrack stopped, but it took a few moments for the automatons to wind down. Their buzzes and clicks slowed and eventually ceased as Larry stared at his own mortified reflection.

"Come now, Larry. Let's not keep Linda waiting."

The Doll ushered him toward the cube containing the fancy bedroom. The camera he'd used earlier stood on a tripod in front of it. Within, Linda lay in in the large four-poster bed, her hair up in rollers, dressed in a baby blue nightgown with a ruffled collar that looked like it was made out of Larry's grandma's doilies. Neither the set nor either of their costumes were from any of the films they'd been in together, at least to Larry's recollection.

"She's still sleeping."

"Galatea awaits her Pygmalion," The Doll said.

Fucking creepy thing to say, Larry thought. *But what does he say that* isn't *creepy?*

The Doll approached the right side of the cube. He removed a key from the same pocket he'd kept the cologne and unlocked the inset glass door. He stepped back and gestured toward the doorway.

Larry approached the cube cautiously. Why didn't he recognize any of this? He'd been in several hundred films, he supposed whatever this scene was could've slipped his mind. But he remembered every film he and Linda had starred in together. He watched them regularly on his big-screen TV, reliving the moments like an erotic highlight reel. Pornography was his home movies. If Ralph Edwards said, "Larry Walker, *This Is Your Life*," the entire broadcast would have to have been censored. The audience would've required rain slickers.

"Action, Larry," The Doll said. He stood behind the camera now, his left eye on the viewfinder.

Larry stepped into the box.

On the bed, Linda's chest rose and fell. She was alive. That was something, at least. Maybe they could hatch a plan while they fucked. If they kept their voices low and their mouths close, The Doll might not even notice. How many conversations had they had while on set that hadn't been caught? Granted, The Doll's camera recorded sound, unlike the 35mm cameras back in the day. But he wasn't wearing headphones. He'd hear whatever was audible through the glass to the human ear.

The door shut behind him. He turned to see The Doll tuck the key back into his pocket.

"Hey!" Larry pounded on the glass. "You never said you'd be locking us in here!"

"I never said I wouldn't." The Doll returned to his place behind the camera. "Please remove your clothes while slowly approaching the bed. Shirt first, socks last."

"Unlock the door and I'll do whatever the fuck you want!"

"It doesn't work that way, Larry. If you don't do as I say you can watch as I remove your costar's skin while she's still alive to feel it. I'll start with her face, work my way down to her beautiful breasts—"

"All right, for fuck's sake!" Larry started lifting his shirt over his head.

"Act like you mean it, Larry." The Doll's voice came over a speaker above the bed. "You've just stumbled across Sleeping Beauty and now you're going to fuck her awake."

Larry tossed his shirt aside and unzipped his jeans, moving toward Linda on the bed. He kicked off the shoes—a pair of scuffed-up Adidas, white with blue stripes—and swaggered toward the bed while tugging down the jeans and undies together, the way he'd always done when the costume required something under the pants. If that wasn't how The Doll wanted it done, he didn't voice his concern.

The socks came off last, one at a time, at the side of the

bed. He looked down at Linda. Her eyes were sunken, puffy and raw from tears. Her face was scrubbed shiny and clean, the rise and fall of the few visible inches of her lightly freckled breasts above the duvet mesmerized him for a moment. He'd been at half-mast as he crossed the room but now he was fully erect, his cock bobbing slightly up and down in time with the pulse of blood to its thick purple head.

He licked his lips. The fake mustache prickled his tongue.

"Get under the covers, Larry."

Larry lifted the blanket. Linda didn't stir. Her eyes didn't move from side to side behind their lids. She wasn't sleeping. Either she was unconscious or she was doing a great job faking it. She'd always been one of the better actors in the porn industry, and in her husband's films she was one hell of a scream queen. It was just as likely she was acting as unconscious.

You can't do this, Larry thought.

You have *to do this*, he told himself. *If you don't, he'll kill you both. But he'll make you watch him kill Linda first.*

Larry raised the covers and climbed over Linda. Again, he wasn't sure if that was The Doll's intent for him but he performed better when working from the left of his costar. A cloud of orange-and-floral scented perfume and light sweat rose as he let the duvet fall over them.

"Caress her breast," said The Doll over the speaker.

Larry watched Linda's eyes for movement. He was so close he could hear her breathing, slowly in and out through her nose. Her lips were thinner than they'd been when she was in her twenties but they were moist and glistening, half parted with the tops of her lower teeth exposed and just the tip of her tongue. His rock-hard rod throbbed against the underside of the blanket, imagining her hot tongue circling the head of his cock, licking the base of it, slurping up his balls.

Fuck, I might just cum right now if I touch her.

Larry reached out and gently cupped her right breast. Warm and yielding, he felt her heart beating beneath his palm. But her breathing didn't change at his touch. Her eyes didn't open. Either she was still out of it or she was doing a hell of a job pretending.

"Linda," he whispered, certain his face was turned far enough from the camera it wouldn't catch the movement of his lips. "Linda, if you're awake move your eyes."

Her eyes didn't stir beneath the lids. Unconscious, then.

"Now kiss her."

The mustache tickled as Larry licked his lips. He leaned over her, opening his mouth, moving closer to hers. He could smell her breath now, acrid and slightly sweet. He imagined his own was worse. When was the last time he'd brushed his teeth? He didn't even know what day it was.

"Squeeze her tit and kiss her."

Larry squeezed her breast and put his lips against hers, not kissing exactly, just sort of mushing them together. Back in their porn days many directors would require them to flick their tongues against each other's, like they were jousting. Larry kept his tongue in his mouth.

Linda's eyes sprang open. She reacted with shock to seeing him on top of her, his lips pressed against hers.

"Larry?"

"It's okay," he whispered into her open lips. "We can figure this out."

She pushed at his arms, trying to shove him off of her, shock turned to anger. Larry held her down, the struggle making him harder. A vague thought that he could reach down between the two of them and jerk up the nightgown and shove it in her before she could stop him arose, but he pushed it away as he held her down. He was no rapist, not even if The Doll forced him to be one.

"We have to get out of here," he said.

"Larry, look out—!"

"I have no guilt in my heart, Larry," The Doll said, not over the speaker this time. His voice came from directly behind him. "Do you?"

Larry's back screamed as he wrenched his head around to look over his shoulder. The Doll had entered the cube while he'd been struggling with Linda. The freak held a black, short-barreled revolver that looked like something out of an old cop movie.

Larry did the only thing he could think to do in that moment: he threw himself over Linda, hoping that if The Doll fired she'd survive the initial blast and have a shot at getting out of here.

He had less than an instant to prepare for the pain. The crack from the pistol and the explosion of fire in his ribcage were simultaneous. For some reason he'd expected one would precede the other, like lightning before the thunder. It was a strange thought to have in the moments before dying.

Linda screamed. She pushed Larry off of her, and he rolled onto his back on the bed, his head propped up by frilly pillows. Two more shots fired. In the glass he saw Linda's body jerk and she fell forward, two dark red holes marring the blue nightgown.

Larry gasped. The hole in his chest whistled, making a sucking sound as he breathed in, like someone giving head.

In the reflection on the glass, he saw images on the two screens above his head. He hadn't noticed anything playing on them before. He'd been too focused on the scene itself. Now he saw that both images were of the same bedroom. Only in one a man and woman he didn't recognize lay dead or dying on the bed. In the other, he and Linda were in a similar state, though in different positions.

On the first, a man in a suit stood with his back toward the camera. On the other, The Doll did the same.

As both the man—The Doll's father, from the video he'd shot when he was a child—and The Doll himself stepped over the beds.

"You're free now," The Doll said. "Both of you."

The Doll and his father raised their pistols to their heads the scene playing out before Larry's eyes faded to black.

"Cut," The Doll said finally. But neither Larry nor Linda was alive to hear it.

12

The Doll—who called himself Jason, though that wasn't his name—dragged the chair over to the Orgy tableau vivant, his "living photographs," though he preferred to think of them as living films. He sat and stared into the cube for a long time, sipping from a tall, cold Harvey Wallbanger, his erstwhile mentor's favorite drink. With the last two human automatons mounted and set in place, he could finally put the past behind him. The final pieces of the puzzle had fallen into place. There was no more work to be done.

Jason picked up the newspaper and reread the headline below the fold, alongside a not-so-recent photograph of Larry: *SECOND FORMER PORN STAR MISSING*. He found it so reductive. As if there was nothing more to a life than what they'd accomplished. The headline for his parents' deaths had read *SOCIALITES DEAD IN DOUBLE MURDER-SUICIDE.* A horrific family tragedy dismissed in a mere six words.

Whirrrr—chug-chug-chug and dead Larry fucked dead Linda doggystyle while the other automatons buzzed and clicked around them, a lifeless, mechanical orgy of cured flesh and oiled metal workings.

The theme of *The Awakening of Mr. and Mrs. S* was "if you can't beat em, join em." This scene was the culmination of that theme, at the climax, so to speak. Linda and Larry had joined the others. They were together again, forever, reenacting their final scene together endlessly.

A happy family. Reunited.

Jason smiled and raised his drink in a silent toast to the men and women who'd made him what he was today, whether they'd know it or not: to his mother and father, to Linda Flint and Larry Walker, to the thousands of actors in hundreds of pornographic films. He smiled, stroking his erection through his pants and sipping the drink, as the scene played again and again and again…

BAIT

When Alexa and I were little and we used fish in the Paintbrush sometimes after school, she'd never had trouble baiting a hook.

Most childhood skills disappear over time if they're not kept up. That particular skill—baiting a hook—it never left Alexa. Maybe if I'd known what she had in mind, I might not have gone to see her the night she texted me. I might have had better things to do with my time. But she'd had that effect on people. A part of me had always wanted to be her, wanted to be *with* her. If I'd been conscious of it, I might have spared myself a lot of pain. Then again, I might have gone to see her anyway.

Once she'd blossomed, men began to gravitate toward her wherever she went. Women, too, though she'd never been with a girl as far as I knew then, which was one of the reasons I never imagined she'd have any interest in me. She didn't need to put on makeup or doll herself up at all. Jogging pants and her hair in curlers, on a brief trip to pick up something from the corner store, some eggs or a chocolate milk, she'd get wolf whistles. She'd get strange men in white vans slamming on their breaks to try and give her a ride. Or to try and get her to give *them* one.

When she did doll herself up—*watch out, sister*. It was like a nature video the way guys would vie for her attention. Trying to be the first to buy her a drink. To chat her up. To take her home.

Alexa and I grew up on opposite sides of the same city, in the same school only because I bussed in. Where I lived, carrying around books like I did got you marked as prey. So, I traveled halfway across the city to her school, where I could pursue academic endeavors without the threat of my five-foot-fuck-all frame getting a beatdown—verbal and physical—from every girl who wanted to prove *they* were the alpha.

After high school, Alexa and I went our separate ways. I stayed to take journalism at a community college. Alexa left town, getting her Masters in Psych at NYU. Nobody had ever expected any less from her. I could have ended up on the street and the kids we went to high school with wouldn't have batted an eye. They all saw me as gutter trash despite my GPO, simply because of where I'd grown up.

I hadn't seen Alexa for a few years since we both went our opposite ways, but we'd emailed each other every so often just to keep up. When I moved to the city for a full-time writing gig that had since fallen through, we tried to get together on a handful of occasions, but circumstance always got in the way, raincheck after raincheck. It got so we were apologizing to each other in those emails more than we were catching up, and it'd begun to feel like a chore—if not for me, certainly for her. Months went by like this. I'd considered just not responding to her last email but of course, sappy me, I did, and Alexa left me hanging, waiting on her reply for *weeks*.

Until one night a few weeks back, she texted me out of

the blue:

I NEED YOU ASAP!!

My blood pressure spiked when I saw those two words in all-caps: *NEED YOU*. I'd seen her brush off so many ostensibly hot guys over the years, from the high school parties to the club scene, the idea of being with her had never even crossed my mind. Okay, not *never*. There was a lonely night or two when my thoughts went back to the two of us skinny dipping at that lake up north and I'd caught a glimpse of her pale slim body in the moonlight. But the thought that she would ever take *me* home—you can imagine how crazy that must have seemed to a Plain Jane like me.

Somehow, I managed to play it cool, even though my heart was drumming in my ears. We were *friends*, after all. Or *had* been. No reason I shouldn't assume she just wanted me to help her move some furniture.

I chose my words carefully. Deleted the text and tried again. I asked her where she was, trying not to seem too eager, trying to play aloof. She had, after all, stood me up the last time we were supposed to meet.

This time she replied back instantly: *my apt pls hurry!!*

I saved the article I'd been working on, a freelance job, and tossed on my jean jacket. The streets were slushy. Some snow remained on garbage bins and trash bags. I'd already walked several blocks in the cold when I realized I'd forgotten my phone—the very thing that had gotten me into this mess—but by then I'd just flagged down a cab and I'd gone too far to turn back. I didn't know at the time how true those words would become.

I wouldn't need the phone, anyhow. I knew where she lived, or at least where she'd lived the last time I'd seen her. If she'd changed her address, well… I'd lived through a lot more embarrassing moments than knocking on the wrong door.

Alexa lived in a townhouse off Amsterdam in Hell's Kitchen. I'd dropped her off there in a yellow cab one night after she'd had a few too many drinks, and the cabbie had continued to my damp, cramped basement apartment in Greenwich, a not entirely unpleasant biographical note I share with the late-great Hunter S. Thompson.

I got out at what I hoped was still Alexa's townhouse, paid the driver, and looked up at the darkened windows as he drove off, the sound of rain slashing under his tires. If she was home, she must have been in one of the back rooms. Otherwise she was sitting in the dark, and I should probably confess, the image of her creamy skin gleaming under the streetlights gave me a thrill.

The second-floor buzzer said KEACH: Alexa's last name. I pushed it and waited to hear her voice. Instead, the door buzzed like an angry insect. I tore it open before the maglock could decide I wasn't worthy of entry—I certainly didn't *feel* worthy right then, especially when I caught site of my reflection in the door glass. I quickly smoothed my hair—a sharp bob in need of a trim—wiped a smear of ink from my cheek and stepped into the small (yet loads bigger than mine!) foyer. From one of the two doors on either side of me, the smell of jerk lamb or goat filled the enclosed space. Even if I hadn't forgotten to eat dinner in my rush to finish the article, I would have been salivating.

Like I said, she knew how to bait a hook.

The stairs creaked all the way up. From the outside, the brownstone gave the appearance of affluence but little of that remained indoors. The wallpaper had peeled, the paint cracked and flecked. Cobwebs covered the wall sconces like handcrafted lampshades, the floors stained and layered with dirt and crumbs as if no one had cleaned in months. At the top of the stairs, Alexa's mailbox was crammed full of envelopes and junk mail. The door number—3—hung upside-down from a single screw. Up here the spicy food smell had given way to the dank stench of someone's clogged sink and/or toilet.

I knocked.

From inside I heard heels cross a wooden floor toward the door, followed by the slight squeak of a rusted hinge I assumed to be the peephole guard. Then the rattle of a door chain, the clack of two bolts unlocking. Finally the door swung open six inches or so while the overhead light in the hall, its dome filled with dead flies, crackled like a bug zapper.

Alexa peered out at me from the darkened apartment. She looked past me, blinking at the cracked stairwell ceiling. "Are you alone?"

"Of course, I'm alone. Alexa, who the hell would I bring?"

She looked over my shoulder again, then nodded and dragged the creaking door halfway open, just enough for me to step inside. I stayed in the hall, suddenly unsure I wanted to be here at all. It seemed like the pungent smell was coming from *inside.*

"Are you gonna come in, or not?"

I thought, *What's the worst that could happen?*

In nights since, I wish to hell I'd taken a moment longer to ponder that.

Because the worst thing that could happen is often far worse than you could ever begin to imagine.

Alexa closed the door behind me and began pacing the room while I tried to acclimate myself to the darkness, everything in silhouette from a streetlamp shining dull yellow through the curtains.

"Alexa," I said, crossing toward her dim, moving shape. Her dark hair had fallen over her shoulders like a hood, much longer than the last time I'd seen her. Back then she'd been trying anything to keep men's attention away from her. One summer, she'd returned to high school with a shaved head. We'd called it her "Sinead" phase. The boys had called her "dyke," which had gotten more under my skin than it had Alexa's for obvious reasons. It was easy for her not to care about labels like that.

"What's going on?" I asked her. "Are you okay?"

The dank smell was stronger in here, though I could also smell a men's cologne, sweat, and the faint flowery talcum scent I'd long ago come to associate with Alexa. As I reached out for her, my shoe struck something soft and solid and I barely managed to catch myself before tripping.

If Alexa hadn't been making me edgy the way she'd kept pacing, muttering to herself the way she was, I might have wondered what I'd hit. My shoe came away tacky from the flooring. With the smell in here, it wouldn't have surprised me to discover I'd stepped in shit.

"I'm turning on the lights," I said.

"*Don't!*" she cried out. She'd stopped moving just long enough for me to make out the fear contorting her features, amplifying my own nervousness. Then right back to pacing, as if the constant movement was the only thing keeping her from jumping out the window.

"Alexa, would you stop clomping around and tell me what the hell's going on?"

"I can't do it anymore," she said. "I *can't*."

"Can't do what, Alexa?" Anger got the better of me. "Would you fucking *talk* to me, already? I came all this way—"

"Okay," she said, seemingly resigned. Her pale silhouette sank with a springy sound into what I assumed must be a chair. "Okay. You can turn on the light."

"Good." I moved back the way I'd come and ran my fingers along the wall. When I found the switch, Alexa said, "Don't scream."

It was a strange thing to say, I mused, as I flicked on the lights. But turning back to her with the light on, I almost did exactly what she'd told me not to.

A man lay on his back on the carpet. Pale-skinned and hairy, his fat, uncircumcised cock stood erect against the mound of his stomach and yellowish pubic hair. His blank eyes stared up at the ceiling. Not blinking. Not breathing. In my shock, I staggered back against the door. The pool of congealing blood surrounding him, spreading out from between his legs, was marred by a single footprint—*my* footprint. My thoughts buzzed with legal terms: *Forensic evidence. Accomplice.* This guy was young, barely older than me. But there was no doubt in my mind he was dead and the stench filling the room had come from him.

Retching, I staggered back, making a home for myself against the door like a frightened spider. I looked up at Alexa. She was watching me closely, gauging my reaction.

"Alexa," I said. I was barely able to look at her with the dead man's prick within my field of vision. It was hard enough to maintain eye contact with Alexa in her lingerie and high heels, like a pinup in some men's magazine—and what the hell had they been doing here, exactly?

"Alexa, were you…? Did you *fuck* this guy?"

She looked at me as if I'd slapped her. I'd struck a nerve, despite my misplaced revulsion. I couldn't explain why my mind had gone there, why the idea of her having slummed it with a man so clearly beneath her seemed more shocking in that moment than the fact that the man was dead. Was it jealousy? Was it insane to feel jealous when the man she'd been screwing lay dead on the floor between us?

I reached behind me, fingers scrabbling for the door handle, eager to leave before Alexa could reel me further in.

"Brook..." she said, the plea in her tone fixing me in place. "*Please*. I need your help."

"What did he do to you? Did he try to... to *rape* you?"

Shame in her red-raw eyes, Alexa tugged at the hem of her high-waisted black panties, as if it had only just occurred to her she was practically naked. She shook her head no.

"What then?" I demanded, struggling to understand, to comprehend the incomprehensible. *She murdered this man*. The notion had finally sunken in.

"It's more complicated than that."

Whatever "it" was, her shock seemed to have subsided. Seeing this made me even angrier. "So, what? You called me here to help *clean this up*, is that it? Haven't had time for me in nearly a year, now you need an errand girl?"

"It's not like you were any more communicative," she snapped.

I needed something to drink. Fear and anger had dried out my mouth, making it difficult to talk—and the *need* to talk, to ask questions, felt compulsive. I moved laterally to the kitchenette, giving the man on the floor a wide berth. Running the cold water, I splashed some on my face, not daring to turn my back on the dead man in the living room.

I caught movement from the corner of my eye but it was only Alexa, standing briefly to snag a glass of red from the coffee table. The glimpse of her bare ass, barely concealed by flimsy, lace-bordered panties, managed to stir feelings in me despite the clear mental image of what must have happened to the dead man. *She killed him*, I thought again. Alexa sat back down, crossed her legs, and downed the glass in one gulp.

I drank greedily from the faucet, then returned to the living room. I sank into her leather sofa, the dead body between us. "Alexa... what the fuck happened? Why did you...?"

The man's penis began to flop.

Not just flop—it was doing a goddamn *jig*.

As we watched, me horrified, Alexa strangely calm, the skin of his penis stretched out, like someone trying to shove their head through a tight turtleneck. I looked up at Alexa. She was eyeing me with a strange look. Curious, as though she was gauging my reaction again rather than reacting to the horror herself. The shock of it was doubled for me. I'd seen two, maybe three penises in my entire life—and certainly none as big or as *excited* as this one.

Suddenly the flesh burst open. Chunks of yellow fatty tissue splattered against the coffee table and the man's testicles oozed out over his freckled leg. I flinched at the sight and managed to hold back a wretch, just glad none of the spatter had landed on Alexa or myself.

Again, movement caught my eye: the black, scabrous legs of an insect. A *large* insect. My reaction to this was more primitive than to the sight that preceded it. I crabwalked over the back of the sofa in horror as the chitinous creature clambered over its host's viscera-splattered thigh and plonked down on the carpet.

I couldn't help myself. I screamed.

Black compound eyes stared into mine as it scuttled toward me on what looked like a dozen legs, tentacles thrashing, its blood-slicked carapace glistening under the lamplight.

Alexa moved quickly, leaping up from the sofa, and stomped down hard on the thing as it reached my feet, where it had been heading straight for what I assumed must have been its destination—my pantleg. Its mucus-like insides squirted out and it squealed like a boiled lobster, writhing under her stiletto heel, its horrible limbs flailing.

She offered me a sympathetic look while she slipped off her shoe, but no explanation. She brought the heel to the kitchen sink, walking awkwardly—one heel, one bare foot—and rinsed the shoe under the tap. I remained where I was, crouched by the door, staring open-mouthed at the mess between my feet. Finally, I managed to put my thoughts into words.

"*What the fuck was that thing?*"

"The males never mature properly," Alexa said over her shoulder, and I wasn't sure I'd heard her correctly at first. "It's best to just put them out of their misery."

"Alexa... what's *happening*?"

"They need hosts," she said, not answering my question. "If they inhabit a suitable host, the relationship is symbiotic. With a non-suitable one... well, you just saw what happens. Paratenic hosts—they don't live long."

I looked at the man on the floor between us, his genitals like a burst piñata of blood.

"Where did it *come* from, Alexa?"

"From me," she said, as if it were obvious.

"You..." I swallowed hard, inadvertently glancing at the lacy material between her legs, pubic hair visible through the fabric. "...that thing was *inside* you?"

She shook her head patiently. "I was born with another living being inside me. A symbiont. *That*—" She pointed to the mess on the floor. "—was one of her brood. Her offspring."

"Why *me*, Alexa? Why did you call me here tonight?"

"I need to confess what I've done. You're the only writer I know."

"How lucky for me," I scoffed.

"And because you're my friend," she added. I saw a deep sadness in her eyes. I tried mightily not to feel sorry for her in that moment, but it was difficult. We'd grown up together. But I wanted more than anything to hate her right now. For what I saw as a betrayal. Not just roping me into a murder, intentional or not, but for making me a witness to this atrocity.

"I wanted you to know about me. Why I've seemed... distant. Why I've held you at arm's length."

"I'm not one of those 'friend zone' assholes, Alexa."

"Of course, you aren't. But you have feelings for me. I've seen it."

I shook my head.

"I have feelings for you, too, Brook. This is what happens to the men in my life. Women, too, if they're incompatible." She jutted her angular chin toward the man on the floor. "*That's* what happens."

"If you knew that, why did you sleep with this bozo?"

"He's not a bozo," she said with a scowl. "He was kind. Besides, it's not like I have the luxury of choice. You've heard of zombie ants?"

I told her I hadn't.

"There's a fungus," she explained. "*O. unilateralis* it's called. It infects the ant's brain, makes it crawl to the top of a leaf blade to spread its spores and infect other ants."

"Okay," I said, not quite getting it. I looked it up later. It's a strange and complicated process, essentially how

Alexa described it except that she'd left out the fact that it kills the zombified ant after the insect reaches the leaf and grows a stalk out of its skull to infect other ants. This is the fungi's *raison d'etre*, a perpetual cycle of mitosis to create endless versions of itself.

"You're saying this… *thing*—this symbiont—that it *controls* you?"

"During its breeding cycle… to a point…" She made a gesture between a nod and a head shake. "…yes."

"It—*she*—made you fu—" I changed tact. "—*have sex* with this—" I almost said *bozo* again. "—with him."

Alexa nodded with a downcast look. "I don't want anyone to die. If I could stop myself—"

"Have you tried to remove it?" I still couldn't think of this thing, this parasite, as anything but an 'it.' My disdain for this 'living being' must have showed because Alexa sneered.

"*She's a part of me*, Brook. Our nervous systems are connected. I can't live without her."

"But it's *killed people*, Alexa. How many?"

She wouldn't look at me. Her gaze was held by the man on the floor.

"*How many*, Alexa?"

"Six," she said, then shook her head. "Ten."

"Ten people."

She was a serial killer. A *multiple murderer*. And here, now, I was her accomplice. It was already far too late to turn back. I considered asking her to turn herself in—but the thought of her in prison broke my heart. That left us with only one choice.

"What did you do with the rest of them? The other…" I didn't want to say it. "…the others like him?"

She told me.

Deep in the woods on the outskirts of Twin Lakes, where Alexa and I grew up, Paintbrush Creek widens to a river. And soon we were on our way in Alexa's Volvo, to the clearing in the woods where we'd baited our hooks as kids. We'd caught plenty of brook trout there, over the years. Late one night, when we were sixteen or seventeen, we'd had a little too much to drink at a bush party and shared our first and only kiss on a park bench carved out of a felled sequoia.

Oh, I'd been hooked all right. From the very first day we met.

All she had to do was reel me in.

During the drive, I'd asked Alexa to tell me everything she knew about her parasite. She hadn't wanted to talk, saying she needed to concentrate on the drive. She said she would tell me afterwards, and I believed her. So we'd listened to the radio while she drove, and every time a set of headlights flashed in the side mirror I worried a cop would pull us over and we'd have to explain why there was a dead man wrapped in a white linen tablecloth in the trunk with his genitals torn to shreds as if he'd slathered them with peanut butter and let a Rottweiler go at him.

At three A.M. we pulled into the gravel lot at the southern entrance to the park. It was over a hundred acres of land, some of it trailed, much of it untouched. The clearing was a bit of a hike. We had a single flashlight and our phones to get there in the dark but it was carrying the body that troubled me. We couldn't exactly drag him without leaving forensic evidence.

Turned out we didn't need to. There was a park maintenance shed that was new since the last time I'd been here. Alexa surprised me by using a couple of bent hairpins to jimmy the padlock.

"Where the hell did you learn that?"

"Remember my parents' liquor cabinet?"

I'd always wondered how she'd gotten into it. Now I knew. She'd been practicing.

Inside the shed were all the tools we'd need. A shovel, a pick, a wheelbarrow, even a bag of lime. It was almost too perfect.

We lifted the dead man out of the trunk and placed him on trash bags we'd laid out in the wheelbarrow. Then we got moving, rolling him into the woods.

This might surprise you, but I've never buried a human being before. When Alexa and I were kids—I think I was about twelve or thirteen—my cat Meowzers died. I cried so much I thought my little heart would burst but when my dad told me I could take her into the backyard and bury her there, I remember I got really quiet. I didn't stop being sad immediately, but just knowing that Meowzers would be there in the backyard, a few feet under the ground, where I could talk to her if I wanted to, it *calmed* me.

We took her to the backyard in a tin box lined with the case for the old pillow she used to sleep on and I helped my father dig the hole. I said something silly as a eulogy I'd probably seen on TV, and together we buried her, under the apple tree. The cement marker my father made is still there in the backyard, only visible when the kid from down the street comes by to mow the lawn.

This was not like that.

For one thing, this guy *smelled.* He stank like rotting vegetation clogging a sewer pipe. The sheet we'd rolled him up in was soaked through with gore and when we finally managed to heave him into the hole, it unraveled, exposing himself to us. Whatever had happened to his body in the time since we'd left Alexa's apartment, under the light of the moon all the veins leading toward his crotch had turned black, the flesh around the wound itself a sort of yellow-green slop.

Alexa climbed down into the hole—she'd put on proper footwear and a tracksuit—and tucked the body back into the sheet.

The body. Just thinking of him like that, like this man was no longer a person, made me sick to my stomach. This was a *human being* in that hole. I didn't know the circumstances leading up to him being in Alexa's apartment and I didn't *want* to know, but even if he was cheating on his wife with a newborn baby at home, this end—a mangled body discarded in an anonymous hole in the woods—it wasn't deserved. And there were ten other people out here, rotting in the earth.

The soil eroded and Alexa slipped climbing out of the hole. She fell face down in the dirt and when she raised her head, she was covered in it: smeared makeup, dirt, blood under her fingernails. That was when Alexa finally broke down crying. When I knelt to console her, she brought her hand to her throat.

When did she get the knife?

"I can't do this anymore!" she said, her voice high and tight, her larynx straining against the edge of the blade.

She was going to kill herself, right in the fresh grave. And there was nothing I could do to stop her. I'd forgotten my phone at home. I'd be burying two bodies instead of one.

I said her name. Sharp as the knife to her throat.

She looked up at me, tears streaking the dirt on her face.

"You don't need to do this," I said.

She sniffled. A runner of snot ran from her right nostril

to her lip. It brought me right back to when we were kids. The time she skinned her knee on our skateboards. The time she'd gotten trashed and picked a fight with a school bully at a party in these very woods, got her ass kicked and came running to me, who hadn't even been invited.

"We can..." I started to say, but I didn't know how to finish. What could we do? "We can figure this out. You don't need to *kill yourself*, Alexa."

"I *do*," she moaned, shaking her head at the dirt. "It won't stop, never, not until I'm dead."

"Or until you give it what it wants."

She looked up, curiosity in her eyes. Still, the knife never left her throat.

"You said the thing inside you, this... symbiont, that it needs a suitable host. *Compatible*."

She nodded, sniffling.

"You're a compatible host. That's why it lives inside you. But what would happen if it found another compatible host?"

She looked at me. Curiosity became realization. "It would breed."

"That's all it wants, isn't it? To breed? To make a perfect copy of itself in some other body. Some other *host*. Has this ever worked for you?"

She shook her head.

"And did the people you... slept with... did any of them know what they were in for? Were any of them *prepared*?" I meant to ask *Did they consent to being violated by a parasite?* but I didn't want to imply she was some kind of rapist. Which was odd, considering she'd been party to multiple murders, involuntary or not.

Again, another head shake, this one almost imperceptible. Ashamed.

"What if..." I didn't know how to say it. How to boil down everything I've wanted for decades into a single question. "What if we tried it? Together?"

She blinked up at me. "You... I could never do that to you, Brook."

"I can't just let you kill yourself. I've... *wanted you...* for as long as I can remember." The shame of never having come out and said it before burned in my cheeks and neck. "You called me, I came. Let me try to help you."

After what seemed like an eternity, she lowered the knife from her throat and started to climb up from the grave. I took her hand and helped her out.

"You understand what that means. If you're incompatible."

I nodded toward the hole in the earth. "I end up in a plot next to—" Here I was about to lay dirt on the man's grave and I didn't even know his name.

"Derrick," she said.

"Next to Derrick," I agreed.

Alexa shook her head. "I would bury you in a special place. *Our* place. Under the old sequoia bench."

Somehow, that was just about the kindest thing anyone had ever said to me.

We went there shortly after we covered over Derrick, Alexa guiding me by the hand through the dark woods, sitting me down on the bench carved into the massive, ancient log. Once, we'd tried counting its rings. We'd lost count but had it figured for at least a century old, likely more.

She sat down beside me. I could barely hold her gaze. This was awkward. We'd been friends forever. Kids together. She slipped her right leg behind me and held me around the waist. I felt her breath hot on my neck, prickling my spine.

From behind, she unsnapped the top button of my jeans. I jerked away nervously. "What are you doing?"

"You'll need to be aroused for this part," she said.

That shouldn't be a problem, I thought. Despite the circumstances and the very real possibility this might be the last sexual encounter I'd ever have—the last *anything*, really—every part of me felt electric. I'd waited for this moment most of my life. I nodded, as imperceptibly as she had earlier. "Okay."

I helped her unbutton me. Helped her slip the jeans off my legs and lay them beside us on the bench. The old wood was cold and slightly damp under my ass but I didn't care. The tips of her index and middle fingers found my clit and began to stroke rhythmically. The electricity streamed down from every part of my body and focused itself on the motion of her fingers. My toes curled. In moments, I was crying out in ecstasy.

In the distance, a wolf matched my cry.

Alexa leaned around and kissed me then, slipping her tongue between my lips. I kissed right back, already exhausted, panting and wet, hungry to taste her but knowing her arousing me was mostly utilitarian, a means to an end.

She stood and pulled down her track pants. Laid them out on the bench, slipped off her underwear and set them beside her pants. She sat on them, beckoned for me to come to her.

I slid over. Alexa put her left leg over my right and pulled me closer, so our bodies were almost touching, and lifted my left leg over her right. I knew the position she was trying to get me into and almost giggled—actually *giggled*—but thankfully managed to hold it in.

"What's wrong?" she asked.

"Nothing," I said. "It's just... lesbians don't actually scissor."

She gave me a calculating look. "Have you ever tried it?"

I'd tried. *Of course,* I tried. I'd gotten myself off using just about every part of my partners' bodies, among other things. But had I ever really given scissoring a fair chance? I shook my head, embarrassed by the admission.

"Then how would you know?"

She had me there.

Alexa took my hands. Drew me in until we were pressed together, her razor stubble grazing my labia. With our lips pressed together—both pairs—Alexa began grinding me. I had to admit it felt quite good, especially with her, though nothing like the stimulation of a hand or tongue. Still, my long-withheld desire for her overwhelmed me and I gripped her ass, her smooth flesh cold as the wood beneath us, pumping my hips, pumping against her ripe mound. I felt her clit hardening against mine, and then...

And then.

I'd only ever been penetrated once by a man. I'd had a boyfriend for a brief period in college, an experiment, so to speak. We'd fucked once, and it had ended almost before it began, with a gooey mess on my belly and an allergic reaction to latex. Of course, I'd used toys of all kinds. Dildoes, vibes, G-spot stimulators. I was inexperienced but I wasn't a *prude.*

This felt nothing like any of those.

Something slick and spongy parted my labia and entered me. At first it felt like a tongue, flicking up and down inside of me, only ribbed and much longer. I freaked out, and nearly pulled away. But Alexa's gaze held me. I stayed fixed to her, and the *thing* inside of her, the *symbiont*, began probing the walls of my vagina, hitting my G-spot like nothing and no one had ever done before.

In moments I came harder than I ever had in my life, this alien creature tongue-fucking me as Alexa's clit rubbed against mine, our thighs intertwined, our bodies so close it was like she was penetrating me herself, and fireworks exploded in my brain as I howled into Alexa's wet, open mouth.

The moment I did, the symbiont must have sensed my full arousal. The tongue-thing was just the tip of it, and with my pussy all but gushing it squeezed itself all the way into me. I felt the *fullness* of it widening me, so large it actually pushed my legs even further apart. I gasped, feeling the flesh split, a wound I'd experience over the next two weeks while sitting, using the bathroom, even walking from my desk to the kitchen and back. I felt the alien *thing* inside me, *filling* me, pressing against my bladder, widening the narrow opening of my cervix and nestling into my uterus. I felt it settling there, making itself cozy, making a home in me.

I expelled the breath I'd been holding in a single burst, my whole body shuddering as I fell into Alexa's embrace.

"She's gone," she said after a moment. There was relief in her voice, but also sadness. Like the miscarriage of a child she'd never wanted.

"What do you mean, *gone*?"

"She's not in me anymore. I can't *feel* her."

She couldn't feel it, because it was in me. *She* was in me. Not just an egg or a copy of itself. The whole symbiont.

And I'd *survived.*

We put our clothes back on in silence. The symbiont felt heavy between my hips but by the time we reached the car, with the wheelbarrow and tools back in the shed, safely locked up, it was like there was nothing there at all. I put in a pad from Alexa's glovebox, the blood from the fissure soaking into it. When she dropped me off at my apartment a few hours later—thanking me, promising to call *soon*, but not kissing me again, leaving me hanging—the wound had stopped bleeding altogether, even though, as Alexa drove off, my heart still was.

Alexa called me several times a week that first month. Wondering how I was doing. How I was handling it. If I thought I'd be okay with the "responsibility." Thanking me over and over for changing her life. After that, the calls grew infrequent. I didn't mind. We'd grown apart, and that was fine. What we'd shared was more important than any short-lived fling might be. Even more than if we'd somehow managed to make the two of us work. We'd been friends for as long as I could remember, but friends often drifted apart, especially if the elephant in the room was far too big to ignore.

I never wrote her story, not as anything I'd ever try to publish. I *couldn't*, even if she'd still wanted me to. The last thing the world needed was another barely disguised parable about the dangers of female sexuality, more sex-negative antifeminist bullshit to pick away at all the progress we'd made over the past century. Even if that story was one-hundred percent fact.

Instead, I did what she could no longer do herself.

When Alexa and I were kids, fishing in the Paintbrush, it took a lot of patience and practice to learn how to bait a hook myself. I pricked my finger countless times, grieved for every lost leech and worm, but eventually I managed to make it work. I remember how proud she'd been of me, that first fish I'd caught—barely bigger than a minnow—once I'd baited the hook on my own.

I had no idea how to pick up a man, or a woman for that matter. But soon it became second nature. I don't know if the symbiont changed me, if it exuded some kind of attracting pheromones while it was in heat or if all I'd ever needed was the confidence boost from finally being with Alexa, finally *getting over her…* Whatever the cause, once those scars healed I felt more sexual, more *in charge*, than I ever had in my life.

Eventually, they were vying for *my* attention.

All I had to do was cast out the line, and wait for someone to take the bait.

PEG

Peg wuddn't a real unicorn, that's the first thing I s'pose I ought to tell ya.

Jed Hapscomb's daughter Rowena May called 'er a "Pegasus" when she come out just a foal with a big ol bone stickin out the top of 'er head—Peg, I mean. After that, the name kinda stuck, even though Peg was actually more like a unicorn than a Pegasus. Hap hisself—that's what folks round here call him, Hap, not Jed—he called the horse "Peg" on all the scrap wood signs he painted by hand and stuck out yonder on the county road, same as the ones pointin back five miles both ways from his farm. Come see the freak o' nature, get yerself some corn or taters on yer way out, maybe a slaba hog if you're feelin peckish.

Cost you five bucks just to see Peg, an ten bucks to pet her. Twenty if you wanna give yer kid a ride and forty for a ride and for Hap to snap yer pitcher with his dead wife's Margaret's Polaroid. In the three years since Peg was born to that old nag who passed giving birth to her—on account o' the rupturin that foal's horn did to 'er lady parts—Hap made more whoring out that abomination of a horse than he did the past five years selling corn and taters and raisin sows, now that's the truth.

Few months after she was born, when the weird protuberance on 'er forehead Hap figgered was some kind of abnormal skull growth actually *kept growin*, he called the vet to take a gander. They brought 'er into Doc Embry's office and got x-rays done of 'er head, an ol' Doc Embry come to find it was cartilage stickin out, not bone. Same as like you got in yer nose an yer ears. Never seen nothin like it before, probably never would again, or so he said.

The second thing y'ought to know is, Peg didn't eat like no normal horse.

That expression bout not lookin a gift horse in the mouth? Doc Embry shoulda never looked inside Peg's. What he found there was damn near more peculiar a sight than that horn of hers.

Turned out them wolf teeth of hers—of which she had six, three on each side—were fully developed at three months old, and sharp as razors. If she'da been conscious at the time o' the examination, she coulda taken a good chomp out of the doc's hand and he mighta lost a finger or two.

But she hadn't been, and she didn't, or Embry woulda likely had to put ol' Peg down and this story woulda turned out a whole lot different than it done.

See, Peg was a carnivore, which is odd for a horse, but them wolf teeth made it easy for 'er to chew up meat. Ol' Happy fed 'er scraps, the stuff the butcher scraped off his pigs' bones after he broke 'em down for the shop. Hoof and cheek and innards. The gray, slimy meat on their curly little tails. Peg enjoyed meat so she ate up every bit Hap slopped in front of her.

Up til then, Hap's little girl Rowena rode all the horses on the farm, but he wouldn't let 'er anywhere near the stable or the pen when Peg was out stretchin 'er legs. He was worried about that horn, you see. As Peg got older that horn didn't just get longer, it got sharper. But second of all it was Rowena who got Peg started on eatin meat, feedin 'er scraps she snuck out from the table. She only admitted to it after the horse got so skinny from not eatin nothin but table scraps Peg woulda died if she kept 'er mouth shut. Rowena, I mean, not the horse. But I guess Peg, too, in the literal sense.

After that, Peg wouldn't eat a damn thing *other*'n meat—no oats, no carrots, not even 'er salt lick. Them shits of 'ers stunk to high heaven. I could smell em from here, now that's the truth, and Hap's farm is a good half mile yonder as you prob'ly seen drivin out here.

Ol' Hap figgered Peg'd take a bite outta them pigs if she had half a chance, and outta Rowena too, if he let 'er near. That's how come when you paid to see Peg she'd have on that grazin muzzle she always wore. Last thing Hap needed was some litigious out-a-towner slappin him with a lawsuit for bitin off one of their kidses fingers, only it turned out that's exactly what he got later on. A lawsuit I mean, not a bit off finger.

I s'pose all that's all besides the point. You're here on accounta what happened to all them city fellas so I'll spare ya my meanderin. Sometimes I forget you big city folk like to cut the bullshit and get straight to the point. Least when it suits ya.

Some local boys, according to the story, they come out drunk as skunks to Hap's farm late one night to do a little cow tippin. Story has it they was out earlier that day to ride Peg, but Hap wouldn't let em on account of they was too big and already reekin o' grain alcohol or 'shine. So they come out again in the dead a night to teach Hap a lesson, or so they thought.

Well, after a couple or three futile attempts to get Hap's bovines to roll on over, one of them boys got the brilliant idea to get Peg outta 'er stall an take that ride Hap wouldn't let em have earlier that day.

They was tryna get the stall door opened, from what I understand, when one of them boys thought it'd be wise to take off Peg's blinders. That was their first mistake. Actually, climbin into that stall was the first mistake. Takin them blinders off was mistake número dos, as them migrant fellas Hap used to hire might say. Hell, let's be frank: that whole night was one big mistake, and them boys was about to find out just about how much.

See, Peg could *smell* them drunk sumbitches, but she couldn't *see* em. And she was a ornery horse, even when she was a filly. Hell, when she was just a foal she done bit the titty off one a Hap's other nags, the one that had a newborn 'round the same time as Peg's mother shat that horned abomination into the world.

They say don't blame the horse, blame the trainer. But in the case of Peg, Hap did just about all he could. Even had a Native American feller come out to try an' break her, but all he done was break his own tibula or fibia or whatever damn bone it was, maybe both.

What's that? Right, I was talkin about them boys started it all, wuddn't I? Ol' gray mare ain't what she used to be. My mind, that is, not Peg. We all know what happened to her. My mind is kinda soupy these days, or so the wife likes to tell me just about every chance she gets, but ain't that the way a things?

Well, okay. One a them boys was already in the stall with Peg, takin off 'er blinders. The other boys was fiddlin with the latch like a couple of virgins tryna unclasp a lady's delicates. That's when Peg starts chasin that first boy 'round the stall like a Benny Hill sketch. He's shriekin and hollerin and Peg's whinnyin and nayin, an finally them other two boys get the latch open, an out he come with Peg hot on his tail.

Turns out one of them virgins musta fancied hisself a rodeo clown instead o' just a reg'lar ol' clown so he starts runnin distraction, and from what everyone saw in the news a week or so later—the same thing that brought all them city fellas out here in droves—you know what happened next.

Them boys said ol' Peg damn near tore that poor boy's soul right outta his body. Say he was ridin 'er like a buckin bronco that night, 'cept he wuddn't holdin on to nothin but the frayin shreds of his own dignity. An' he weren't sittin on no saddle, he was horn-deep up the keister right on Peg's forehead with 'er eyes rollin around in 'er head like she needed a damn exorcist, and his own just about poppin outta his skull.

Well, it was about that time Hap come out with a rifle and a lantern, and suffice to say he was decidedly unhappy 'bout what he saw. 'Cordin to him, them two virgins was holdin hands with their recently deflowered friend while Peg bucked and brayed, reamin out his anal canal like a core drill, as the French say.

After a while, Hap managed to get the ornery ol' girl settled down nuff so the three a them could pry the boy's tarhole off'n Peg's horn, which was slick with shit and blood and undigested bits of what the boy likely had for supper that night. Boy was bleedin pretty good too, like a stuck pig accordin to Hap, who ought to know considerin he slaughtered his share of em in his time.

Hap brought out some cotton balls an a rag an bucket, an told them boys to warsh up Peg's horn and to pack their friend's ass crack so he didn't bleed to death, probably in that order. Said he'da done it hisself 'cept he wanted to teach them a lesson their daddies shoulda taught em a long time ago. That lesson bein, you don't mess with a man's livelihood, 'specially if that livelihood's a grumpy ol' nag with a horn on 'er head.

Well, them boys left the Hapscomb farm reekin o' shit with their tails tucked 'tween their legs—and a wad of blood-soaked cotton between one of em's. Hap promised he wouldn't say peep to their folks but lo and behold one of them boys had to run his big mouth, and it ended up the mother of the boy who lost his anal virginity to a horse with a horn on 'er head decided it'd be in 'er best interest to sue ol' Hap for every penny he had to his name.

Come to find out, Hap didn't have much money to give 'er, which come as a surprise to no one apparently except for the virgin's mama. The farm'd barely broke even back then, what with the goddamn Democrats cuttin subsidies an' all. Still, what Hap made whorin out Peg kept em afloat, and that boy's folks knew that much, at least.

Somehow or th'other, the local rag got wind of all this and published the story—probably the same one that got you interested all them years ago. Letterman read about it on his show, made a worldwide laughin stock outta them boys, and got a lot of folk drivin all the way out from the city to see the horse that done it, to see Peg and get their pitcher took with a "genuine unicorn."

Business was boomin after that. And Judge Crawford done threw the lawsuit outta court, said if them boys hadn't gone out to Hap's farm stinkin of shine an' provokin Peg, she'da never assaulted him in the anus.

Now I believe they call that "blamin the victim" these days, but back then it was just plain ol' common sense not to poke a bear. Course, nobody woulda expected a lady horse to penetrate the anal pucker of a teenage boy but there you have it. Stranger things, an' all that.

It was 'round this time the government come a-sniffin aroun, as they do. They smelled money, and untaxed money at that. Turns out, Hap hadn't been filin his taxes since his wife passed. Owed em more than he could pay with his earnins, and if he didn't make that money back quick the bank was fittin to foreclose on the farm, or as Hap put it, they was "fittin to bend him over an go in dry." Add to that a li'l girl smart enough to eventually go off to college someday, an Hap found hisself in quite the conundrum.

That's where you come in, I guess. This *documentary* you're makin bout them city fellas and what happened to em, not that I have much sympathy.

Now, I ain't the judgin kind. Leave that happy horseshit to the Almighty, is my credo. But any o' them fellers come out here lookin to get cornholed by a filly with a horn, I figure they got what's comin to em. Now poor Hap was in a tight spot, and I know he done what he had to do to get his ass unstuck, so to speak.

But Lord I cannot begin to fathom the horrors he musta seen when them city fellers come a-hollerin. I know they showed them tapes at his trial. Damn thing was a three-ring circus, includin the horse tricks. They never showed em on the news, mind. Always had em blurred out, which considerin the content was pro'lly for the best. Alls I know is you could hear ol' Peg whinnyin like a horse in a burnin barn, and all them fellers groanin and moanin while they used that damn demon horse's head to get their jollies off.

Now Sheriff Deacon an me go way back. That poor sumbitch had to watch every damn one o' them tapes 'fore he turned em in for state's evidence, and his face was still green when he passed on what he saw to yers truly. Ghastly stuff, I can tell you that much. Stuff that'd make ya sick just to think bout.

I tell ya, I seen my share of farm animals ruttin. Hell, back when I was a boy bout the same age as them kids from the beginning, I seen a feller stick his pecker in a cow's cooter. The abominable stench that wafted over from that unholy congress nearly made me upchuck my lunch, but it's the God's honest truth. Now the Bible says thou shalt not layeth with a beast as thou layest with a woman, but it don't say nothin about doggystyle, and it sure as shit don't say nothin bout gettin it up the cornhole from no horse with a horn.

Ol' Hap, all he done, or so he says, was keep a hold on Peg's reins while them boys slipped off their kicks and took turns easin their hairy assholes onto that horn. Some other feller, the guy who wore the hangman's mask in them videos, recorded it all for posterior like it was Christmas mornin. Hap says he tried to think o' nothin but the money, which meant he'd be able to hang on to his livelihood and make a decent life for Rowena May. This business, though, it was *anythin* but decent. Fella with the hangman mask was the one who paid him. Hap got to thinkin it was sumpthin like them big city fellers who pay a ridickless amount o' cash just to shoot wild animals in a pen. And this feller in the hangman mask, he was the ringleader, takin a hefty cut 'fore Hap saw any money at all.

That in mind, Hap got to wonderin, while he held Peg back from murderin them boys via the rectum—which reminds me o the punchline to that ol' joke: "Rectum? Dang near killed 'im." But ol' Hap, holdin on to them reins an holdin back his gorge from the stink o' human excrement—funny how you get used to all manner of animal shit but people shit don't ever seem to get any less foul. I s'pose there's a lesson in that. Anyways, ol' Hap starts a-wonderin just how big a cut the Hangman was takin, an' if'n he kept that cash on his person or elsewhere.

But Hap don't act on that thought this time. This time he just holds them reins tighter than his pecker when he's holdin in a piss with them kidney stones he had a while back, an he keeps his eyes shut to stop hisself from pukin while them city folk took turns ridin Peg's horn.

Now I should mention, Hap never had much love for that horse. Way he tells it, he done put a rifle to Peg's head more'n once an willed hisself to pull the trigger. He knew she was an abomination just like the rest of us. But he says he stopped short at the last minute on account of, a) despite bein a horse, Peg also happened to be a *cash cow*, and b) Rowena loved the thing, even though she weren't allowed to ride 'er.

Still, that night Hap found hisself sympathizin with that retched nag. Watchin all them city boys take off their weddin rings 'fore they pulled down their underpants made him realize this was more than just an unholy covenant between Man and Horse. This was *rape*, pure and simple, not unlike if them fellas was stickin their willies in Peg's holiest of holies. And it was clear, the way the ol' gal whinnied and neighed, them eyes rollin around in 'er head while them fellers eased their puckers down on that horn, deeper and deeper, that ol' Peg had no interest in bein part of it.

Up til then, Hap had made his peace with the fact he was pimpin out Peg's horn to them perverts. But Peg was a lot more'n just 'er horn. Folks who been around 'er long enough for their kid to take a ride or have their pitcher took, they didn't see the same things Hap did. Peg was strong-willed, too.

And she was *teeth.*

That's when Hap come up with his plan.

Damn sure wuddn't the smartest of plans, as far as plans go. But Hap wuddn't exactly the smartest o' fellers. Come from a long line of pig farmers and not much in the way of schoolin. He aimed to change that for Rowena May. She was doin pretty well for herself at the public school despite the handicap of bein born to a mental midget like Hap. But she had 'er mother in 'er too, an 'er mother'd been one of the smartest gals in town, which was why it come as such a shock when Margaret Ellis became Margaret Hapscomb. Folks who knew 'er said it was to spite 'er daddy. But they're both gone now, so who can say for sure?

What's that ya say? Well, that is odd, can't say I ever thoughta that. Always seemed peculiar that Peggy was short for Margaret, wuddn't ya say? Prob'ly don't mean nothin in this partic'lar situation but it sure is a odd coinkidink just the same.

Anyhoo, to make a long story a might bit shorter, Hap decided that very night if he was gon' take any more of the Hangman's money he'd let Peg have a go at em. Nip em in the butt, if ya catch my drift.

Next night come round, and out come the Hangman with a busload a horny idiots. All of em had on them li'l Zorro face masks to protect their identities if the tapes ever got leaked, just like the night before. This was a while before the TicketyTok an all that, but shit like that seem to make its way to the public eye anyways, don't it? Like maybe it's too terrible to keep secret. Like the universe or Fate or some other hippy-dippy shit *wants* people to see em.

So just like the last time, Hap straps Peg down with 'er

blinders an grazin muzzle on. An as them city slickers get their puckers nice and slick with the lube the Hangman passed around, little do they know that this time Hap lef one of them buckles on the muzzle loose.

The men all had their skivvies off by the time the Hangman brought Peg's head low enough for the first feller to climb atop. Hap watched this time, despite how disgusted he was by the whole ordeal he'd found hisself caught up in. He watched an he bided his time. He said those deviants were tuggin on their willies and squeezin their balls, just a-waitin on their turn. Meanwhile, the prevert on the horn was ten-inches deep, ridin up and down, them eyes o' his rolled back in his head.

I don't wanna say what happened next, but I believe it was the proverbial straw that done broke the camel's back, the camel bein ol' Hap and the back bein the limit of his tolerance.

So what Hap done was simply flick the buckle. The muzzle come loose just as the first of them sickos shot his wad in the dirt, and ol' Peg turned her head and bit that Hangman feller's hand clean off.

Well, it was bout that time the Hangman started screamin, holding on to his wrist tryna stem the geyser o' blood, while Peg jerked her head up, lifting the feller on her horn, skewerin him up to his lungs. Meanwhile, at least accordin to the video they showed at the trial, and what Sheriff Deacon related to me prior to that three-ring circus, Hap stepped back and let go of the reigns and let nature take its course, as the French say.

Well, Peg took the opportunity to leap forward, the feller on her horn floppin around on the top o' her head like a droolin idiot on a mechanical bull. Coroner said he was dead prob'ly the second he took that horn all the way to the hilt. 'Course that didn't stop him from havin a hardon that'd shame a porn star. Th'other fellers knew their time was up and got to runnin, only half of em had their pants 'round their ankles, an tripped on em the second they started, fallin face-first in the hay n dirt. One feller did a faceplant in a heap o' Peg's shit, an he was one of the lucky ones.

Now Peg went right for the closest feller's pecker, chomped the sumbitch right off. But she didn't eat it. Figure she was too riled up to eat. The guy dropped like a gunny sack full o' corn and Peg kept chargin on ahead. One feller thought he was clever. Took off his red T-shirt and started flappin it like a matador. I s'pose he was tryin to distract 'er, but she ran right at the dumb sumbitch and took a good chunk out of his ass 'fore he managed to climb over into the sow's pens.

Peg got one of the fellers on the ground before he could stand back up. Bit off half the poor sumbitch's face. I can scarcely imagine the last thing that feller musta seen, Peg's jaws closin in on him with all them sharp teeth while the dead man with the hardon hung over him, arms and legs akimbo.

Now them other fellers, they went runnin from the barn hither and thither. The smart ones ran for the bus, 'cept the Hangman held the keys, and he was passed out from blood loss. Hap claimed at the trial he didn't want no one to get hurt. Now I can't speak on whether or not that's the God's honest truth but I do know while Peg was distracted, he climbed out a winduh and went to get his rifle.

He said it was time to put that ol' nag outta her misery.

Peg, in the meantime, went after them fellers runnin out the barn with their pants still unzipped. She was voracious, gallopin back and forth, hungry for blood, hungry for *revenge*, the dead feller with a hardon still bouncing around on her head like a kid on a carousel.

"Stay in the house, Rowena May!" you could hear Hap shout on the tape, over the screams and whinnies and cries for help. "*PEG!*" he shouts then.

On the tape you can hear the horse neigh, almost like she's talkin back.

"This is for your own good!" Hap shouts then.

That gunshot cut through all the screams. *PA-POW!*

You could hear Peg whinny then, but accordin to Hap he just winged 'er an she went off runnin, gallopin down the drive to the county road.

Hap hoofed 'er into that rusty ol' pickup o' his and drove off after 'er. Come to find out she made it all the way to town by the time he caught up. Peg was gallopin like Seabiscuit down Main Street. Some folks who saw 'er said they thought she was a blood-streaked Sagittarius. You know, the Zodiac sign an all.

What's that? A center? Oh, a cen*taur*? Well, okayden. Whatever them thing's is called, that's what they said. Folks didn't see Peg's head at first, ya see, her runnin at a gallop. Just Peg's body with a man perched on top, his free willy flopping back and forth like a conductor's wand at Carnegie Hall. An those same damn fool kids who set this whole ordeal into motion was smokin reefer outside the pool hall, an likely thought "there but for the grace o' God go I," or whatever the modern yo-yo equivalent is.

Hap chased Peg all the way to the center o' town, an while she trotted right up the town hall steps an swung her head 'round, flingin that dead naked feller right through the front winduh, almost like she was makin some kind of formal protest, Hap jumped out the truck and lined up his shot.

Ol' Mayor Burton come to the winduh just about then

and seen that blood-drenched nag snortin and sneerin out on the steps. Likely figgered Peg was a Horse of the goddang Apocalypse come to tell him his time was up, 'til he seen the naked feller sprawled out at the foot of the front desk like he done dropped dead from priapism on his way to payin his property tax. An he mighta seen Hap standin out front of his truck, if Peg herself hadn't been in the way.

But she was, an it was the crack of the rifle that signaled Hap's presence. Then her head burst open like one o' them Mexican peenatas, only instead o' raining candy on Burton, the litigious sumbitch got painted with blood and brains, an pelted by the sharpest damn horse teeth anyone ever seen. Out on the campaign trail, Mayor Burton liked to make a point 'bout how he wuddn't afraid to get his hands dirty, but I can't he'p but wonder how he felt bout gettin the rest of him covered in the stinkin insides of a dead nag. Not too favorably, is my guess.

Well, Hap got the job done finally but his part in this song and dance was far from over. They say a feller who represents hisself in court's got a fool for a client, and never has that been more accurate than at Jed Hapscomb's trial. I s'pose y'all know he's servin five to ten at Nebraska State Penitentiary for animal cruelty and criminal negligée causin death, o' that Hangman feller an the human half of your centaur, them an a couple others. Feller without a face survived, by some miracle or trick o' the Devil. But who would want to, seein what he seen?

Bank took the farm a short while later, and Rowena May got took in by her grandmama. Better off than with her halfwit father, most folks agree, 'specially after the trial. Nowadays, folks round here, when someone fucks up, they call it a "Peggin." Feller blows up his trailer cookin meth, he got Pegged. Mayor's wife caught cheatin with their undocumented gardener, all three of em got a Peggin.

Now I wish I was the type of feller who could sum all this up for you folks like some shaggy dog story with a pithy comment or a clever one-liner, but truth is that just ain't me. Save it for the barstool philosophers down at the Tartan Tap, is my credo. Heck, maybe y'all can give the story a spit shine in that documentary o' yers. That'd be real nice.

What you said 'bout Peg bein short for Margaret got me thinkin, though. There was a time when Mags was alive an Hap used to come to me to gripe 'bout how she was gon' "nag him to an early grave." Turned out 'twas a nag horse just 'bout put him there instead.

And I can't he'p but wonder, if Mags hadn't gone early to the grave herself if'n all that Peg stuff never woulda happened. She prob'ly woulda put the horse down when Peg was born, I figger. Better to put it out of its misery quick than let the poor beast suffer as a carnival freak. Mags was a sensitive soul that way. Even if she hadn't, she likely never woulda let those city fellers take turns ridin on that horn. Or if she had, she woulda had the brains to get the Hangman's money up front an take a steeper cut.

Makes ya think though, don't it? 'Bout how close any of us might be to a Peggin of our own? Metaphorically speakin, of course.

Really makes you think.

AUTHOR NOTES

Well, here we are, at the end of another collection—though you may have noticed this one was a little lighter than the last three. Not in tone, but in page count.

Originally I'd intended to release the novella *Skin* on its own, but I struggled with the title. I still don't *love* the title. It's bland, for one thing. It says nothing. Often I start with a title and write a story around that, but sometimes it's an image I'm struck with—in this case, it was the gruesome tableau in the climactic scene. After I completed the gamebook *Try Not to Die at Ghostland* (due for release from Vincere Press sometime in 2023), I couldn't get that image out of my head. Generally I flounder in the days and weeks following a completed novel, skipping from one idea to the next. This time, I knew exactly what I wanted to write. I *had* to write it, to purge that image from my mind.

My struggle with the title (I went through several: *Skin Flick*, *Skin Dolls*, *The Doll*, *The Doll Killer*, *Tableau Vivant*, etc.), and its slightly-shorter-than-*Woom* length, made me decide I should add a few stories I'd been wanting to release along with it to beef up the page count. "Bait" had been previously published in 2021 in Matt Shaw's *Battered, Broken Bodies* anthology. And "Peg," at the time I finished writing *Skin*, only lacked an ending.

My good friend Danika who admins the Woomies Facebook page had been pushing me to finish "Peg" for a while, but I just couldn't get the ending to work in my head before putting it to "paper." It was the first short story I'd tried writing since "Bait" in 2020, and I was woefully out of practice. The narrator's voice was giving me a bit of trouble, too. I was sure I'd be forced to banish it to the Land of Unfinished Stories. Fortunately after I finished *Skin* I came back to it with fresh eyes, invigorated by the prospect of finally birthing that equine abomination into the world.

"Bait" was a story that went through many incarnations before becoming what it is now. Truth be told, the original setup of the old friends meeting was how I'd begun an earlier story—"How to Kill a Celebrity," from *Video Nasties* in 2017. I loved the idea of someone passing down a curse to a friend who secretly wants to be more, and couldn't shake that kernel of a concept. Three years later I turned it into "Bait." I'll leave it to you to decide whether it worked or not.

And now, the part where I thank people. Thanks go first to my amazing wife, for suffering through the kind of stories she might not normally read to give me necessary and brutally honest feedback, and also for putting up with having to listen to me rattle off these weird and twisted ideas in the first place. Thanks as well to first readers Danika Meyerson and Anna Reid, whose comments and friendship are invaluable.

And thank you to all the Woomies, whose interactions with me and one another make me smile on a daily basis. I'm incredibly honored to have helped foster a little online community where people can laugh about gross stuff and talk about serious stuff, while sharing our love of reading the darker side of horror fiction. Thank you all for being a part of my life!

D.R.
November 2022

For more delicious dark fiction,
visit **www.duncanralston.com** and
www.shadowworkpublishing.com.

Made in the USA
Las Vegas, NV
26 April 2023